I0557249

TIME CORRIDOR

WHISPER PROJECT

Edited by Tiffany S. DeBrosse and Michael Shaw

A PWG Anthology published by Viral Cat Press

Published by Viral Cat Press
San Francisco, CA

Copyright © 2024 Viral Cat

ISBN-13: 979-8-9911641-0-8

Printed in the United States of America.

"We all have time machines, don't we? Those that take us back are memories, and those that carry us forward are dreams."

– H.G. WELLS

INTRODUCTION

Time Corridor: Whisper Project is an anthology containing eight authors' works. Conceived in the Pitman Writers' Guild, the anthology's original premise was that each author place the word "whisper" in their respective story. Soon, the collection evolved with surprising nuance. Each piece features a character from another, and these arcs are explored in the past, present, and future. The collection embraces the uncanny, with tales of magical realism, science fiction, and tragedy creating a literary landscape in which the reader may reflect on the boundaries between reality and perception, as well as the impact of cultural and temporal contexts on decisions, beliefs, and experiences.

Acknowledgements

Time Corridor: Whisper Project wouldn't be possible without the support, contributions, and inspiration of the Pitman Writers' Guild. Special thanks to Mira A. Frost and Fay W. Tinsley for the anthology's beautifully haunting artwork. Many thanks to my co-editor, Michael Shaw, whose editorial insight has been essential in bringing this anthology to life. And lastly, thank you to each and every author whose work graces this anthology—I am in awe of your stories' weave and punch.

ACKNOWLEDGEMENTS

TIME CORRIDOR

WHISPER PROJECT

TIME CORRIDOR

WHISPER PROJECT

D. W. Oravic

LOVE BEYOND FEELING

Molly carefully placed the last slice of French Toast on the plate. Four thick slices tiered in a tight curve, a golden brown mountain studded with individual mint leaves, each stem precisely placed into holes delicately made with a toothpick. A fine snow of powdered sugar coated the landscape, broken up by rivulets of maple syrup that pooled around the base. It was a culinary masterpiece. She inhaled deeply, the sweet fragrance of her creation inviting feelings of homey comfort that refused to answer. Molly was on the verge of tears.

She took another deep breath, pushing the fear and anguish down inside, then turned with a forced smile and set the plate in front of Rick. His eyes locked on to the French toast, yet his face remained as vacant as it had been since the accident. Molly watched as he ate. Each cut of the knife was made with intent, each bite taken at a regularly paced interval. Occasionally chewing noises escaped his mouth.

Molly stood with bated breath in anticipation, hoping for the smallest indication of enjoyment or pleasure. But there was not a single happy noise to be heard. Rick finished the plate with efficiency. Not a crumb or a drop of syrup found its way off the plate onto the table. Then he burped. Molly jumped in surprise, hope rising in her chest. Was he expressing satisfaction?

"What do you think?" she asked, the hope in her chest expanding like a balloon reaching the upper atmosphere, straining against its thin latex walls, threatening to burst at any moment.

"It was sweet. And eggy. The mint made my mouth cool," he replied, his words flat and lifeless.

"It's your favorite food," Molly reminded him.

"I remember that, but the memories don't make sense. It's adequate for my nutritional needs. You spent a lot of unnecessary time preparing it."

The bubble of hope in Molly's chest deflated, replaced by bitterness.

"Because I love you," she said with an edge, a month of anger and sadness coalescing into a venom that caught her off-guard.

"To love someone is to waste time? I remember wasting time on you, but I don't know why. So little about my past makes any sense. I feel like…like there's a whisper of the reason in my mind, but I can't comprehend it. Like when I tried to explain calculus to Sandra."

After four weeks of this, there was nothing that Rick could say that would shock her, yet she still fixated on several of his words. Waste. A word with baggage. A word that has its roots in disdain. Feel, a word linked with emotion. Yet Molly detected no links. Each word was like a paralyzed limb, keeping its appearance while being severed from the body and rendered lifeless.

It was too much. The French toast had been her last great attempt to reach him, yet it had failed like her other efforts. A dam of pent-up frustration burst inside her, and with a cry she swept his empty plate onto the floor. The plate made a dull cracking sound as it hit the tile, followed by a higher pitched shatter. Rick watched the whole episode passively. Molly didn't even see him blink.

"Jesus, Rick, what the fuck did they do to you?" Molly sobbed. She threw herself down in the chair across from him and rested her face in her arms, trapping her tears and smearing them.

"Dr. Moss was very clear about the procedure," Rick said. "I was dying and put into an induced coma until my body healed. Then they revived me."

Molly sat up and wiped her arms dry on her jeans. "No, they didn't revive my Rick. I don't know what the fuck you are."

"I'm Rick," he stated flatly.

"The fuck you are. I'm going out. Make Sandra dinner when she gets home from school."

***

"Dad."

Rick looked over from the recliner he'd moved into after Molly left. CNN was on the television. A small human girl was standing next to him.

"Sandra," he replied.

"I need you to sign this," she said, shoving a plastic folder onto his lap.

"You should specify what you want me to sign to avoid ambiguity," he said, opening the folder.

"Why? You know where to sign. Less words are e-fish-ant. You said that yourself."

"In a repeatable context, yes. But I sign your folder on Fridays. Today is Tuesday. This is out of the ordinary, so therefore, must be different."

Sandra raised the right side of her nostril in an exaggerated sneer. "Same shit, different day."

She held the sneer for a moment, but on the inside, Sandra was as excited as if she'd put a firecracker inside a soda can.

"Molly would be cross with you if she heard you say that word," Rick said.

"But mom's not here, and you don't care. Shit shit shit shit shit shitty shit shit shit," Sandra exclaimed gleefully, balling her hands into fists and hopping from one foot to another with each expletive.

"They're just words," Rick replied flatly, turning his attention back to the folder. He opened it up, revealing a disciplinary report. "You punched a boy in the crotch," he said after reading it.

"Johnny Booger wiped a booger on my sleeve. I almost barfed," she replied, leaning on the arm of the chair and swinging her legs to each side making the whole recliner shake.

"I doubt that's his real name," Rick said.

"It should be," Sandra replied.

"What punishment did you receive?" Rick asked.

"I had to sit out in the hall for the rest of class, and they sent this letter," she said, ceasing her swinging and standing up straight.

"Did you gain more from the assault than you lost from the punishment?" he asked.

"I think so…not sure. What do you think?" she asked.

"A booger is just dirt and mucus. Would you have hit him if he'd wiped a ball of mud on your sleeve?"

"This is different! His booger was red and green and brown too. And the other kids all pointed at me," she said with a frown, reliving the event again in her mind.

Rick thought for a moment. "So, by placing his booger on your sleeve, he made you an object of derision?"

Sandra had no idea what derision meant, but it didn't sound good. She nodded.

"That makes no sense to me, but very little does any more. Did they stop pointing at you after you hit him?"

Sandra nodded.

"And there's to be no further disciplinary action?"

Sandra shook her head.

"Then it was worth it." Rick signed the sheet and handed the folder back to her.

"Yes!" Sandra declared, pumping her fist in triumph. "I knew you'd understand. Not like mom."

"Molly seems to be irrational most of the time," Rick agreed.

"You don't love us anymore," Sandra said with a blunt delivery rivaling her father's, yet her clasped hands and twisting foot belied the sudden pain that had welled up inside of her.

"I don't understand the concept of love," Rick said.

"But you did before the accident," Sandra pointed out.

"So the evidence suggests, but I can't make any sense of my past behavior regarding what you call love."

"So you don't hate us either," she said, her voice lifting a bit with her spirit.

"Another foreign concept."

"So you're not going to leave us?"

"It's possible that Molly will become so cross with me that she'll make me leave, but I have no reason to leave on my own accord. The accommodations are more than adequate."

"You think mom will kick you out?" Sandra said, her heart suddenly racing with panic.

"I can't say. So far, she's the one that keeps leaving."

***

The Top Deck was your typical family-run sports bar and restaurant. Big screen TVs adorned the walls everywhere you looked, and the menu stopped just short of being one of those diner menus that had so much food on it that it left you paralyzed with indecision. Not that Molly was eating. When Jennifer Stanz found her, Molly was nursing a rum and Coke, sitting in a booth as far away from the other patrons as possible, facing the wall. Jen slid in across from her.

"Molly, you look like shit. What's going on? Is it Rick?"

Molly nodded, then put her face into her hands and began to sob.

"Jesus," Jen said, waving the waitress away. "It's three in the afternoon and you're drinking. How long have you been here?"

Molly shrugged.

"Come on, hun, what's going on?" Jen asked, grabbing one of Molly's hands away from her face and holding it tightly in both of hers.

"Rick's dead," Molly sobbed.

Jen froze in surprise. "Oh my God, Mol...When? He was doing so well."

"He's been dead since the accident. That thing in my house is just an animated corpse."

"I know he was brain damaged, or something wasn't right, but it's that bad?" Jen asked.

"That's just it, Jen. He's not brain damaged. They did a whole slew of scans on him after they woke him up. There's nothing physically wrong with him."

Jen shook her head. "So what's his issue?"

Molly sighed, wiped her eyes and took a drink. "Rick's not there anymore, ok? He has no emotions. He's like a robot. He has all of Rick's memories, but doesn't understand them."

Jen's face scrunched in confusion. "What does that mean?"

"Like, it said it has no idea why it married me. That all its memories of our time together seem irrational."

"Ouch. What a fucker. Why would he say something so horrible? You sat at his bedside twelve hours a day for weeks after the accident."

"Because it's true. When I told him how much time I spent with him in the hospital, he told me that it wasn't a very efficient use of my time."

"What a prick," Jen said, flagging down the waitress and ordering a beer.

Molly finished wiping her tears with a napkin and tossed it down onto the table. "For him to be a prick, he would have needed to say it out of malice. He's not capable of malice. Like I said, he's not capable of any emotions at all."

"You said that you two, you know," Jen formed a circle with her left thumb and index finger, then moved the index finger of her right hand in and out rhythmically.

Molly rolled her eyes. "Are you five years old?"

"What five-year-old knows the fucking gesture? I'm at least eleven," Jen retorted, taking her beer as the waitress put it down and sipping it.

"Yes, we did. And his dick worked, and he enjoyed it, but it was mechanical. I had to tell him to do it, and he's never expressed any interest in doing it again. It was like riding an organic dildo saddle."

"So, no connection," Jen said.

"Yes! No connection. His enjoyment was purely physical. And do you know what I walked in on him doing in the bathroom?" Molly asked, a disgusted look on her face.

"I'm assuming not what I instantly thought of," Jen said.

"He was licking the inside of the fucking toilet bowl," Molly said, pushing the rest of her rum and Coke away.

Jen gagged. "What the fuck? Oh my God. What the hell for?"

"He said he remembered hating cleaning the toilet more than anything in the world, so he figured if anything could induce an appropriate emotional response in him, it would be that."

"Dear God. I think I'm going to throw up," Jen said. "I guess since he actually did it, it didn't work."

"He said he noted the possibility of contracting an E. coli infection, but had no feelings of disgust," Molly said with a shrug.

"I can't. I just can't," Jen said, pushing her beer away. "I'd have thrown him out of the house. I wouldn't be able to look at him after that."

"Now you know what I'm living with," Molly said in resignation.

"How is Sandra taking it?"

"Sandra toys with him. She treats him like a plaything. He's a father that will do anything you ask and doesn't give a shit."

"When you put it like that, it doesn't sound like a bad thing. Who doesn't want a man around that will do anything you ask and won't give a shit? Toilet licking aside."

"That's not the fucking point," Molly snapped.

"What's the point then?" Jen asked.

"The point is that Rick is dead, and his corpse is living in my house. How 'm I supposed to grieve, Jen, when I see him every day? Every time he speaks, I'm reminded he's dead all over again."

"Ok, look, just because the doctors can't find anything wrong with him doesn't mean he's dead. What if you just treat him like he has Alzheimer's? They have support groups for that."

"People with Alzheimer's have the courtesy to forget who you are instead of knowing exactly who you are and not giving a shit."

Molly sighed and finished her rum and coke. Nobody understood what she was going through. She could tell Jen was trying to understand. Maybe she would if she had some time to let the implications soak in. But that didn't offer Molly any comfort now.

"What does his doctor say? You said he was some kind of trauma specialist," Jen asked.

"He doesn't know. He has no fucking clue."

Jen became thoughtful. "Maybe you need to consult with someone else. I have an idea."

***

Rick stood at the sink, slowly filling a measuring cup repeatedly and pouring it into a pot.

"Dad, you don't need exactly six cups of water to boil the macaroni," Sandra said.

"If the box says six cups, there must be a reason for it," Rick replied.

"Dad," Sandra said, staring at him.

"Yes?"

"You said you remember things from before, right?"

Rick paused his water refill and nodded.

"So, you *know*, from experience, that you don't need six cups of water."

"They wouldn't say six cups if it wasn't important. Perhaps the noodles taste better with six cups."

Sandra continued to stare him down, then had a thought. "You tell mom a lot that she wastes her time on illogical things. You know that you don't need to stand there like a freak measuring out six cups. The noodles don't care. I don't care. *You* are wasting *your* time."

Rick considered her words, put the measuring cup down, and took the entire pot to the sink and added water, eyeballing it the rest of the way.

Sandra smiled. "See? If you want mom to let you stay here, you need to stop being a freak and start trusting your memories."

Rick nodded, appearing thoughtful. "Don't use that word. It's hurtful," he said, but neither his tone nor manner belied any hurt.

"Ok, dad, sorry," Sandra said, joy surging through her.

Rick turned on the burner and poured the macaroni into the cold water, defying the directions to wait until it came to a roiling boil, then sat at the table with Sandra.

"You've been reveling in my condition for weeks. Just today you were swearing at me and appeared to enjoy it. You know I'm not hurt by that word. Why did you capitulate?"

Sandra shrugged, but answered. "If pretending keeps you here, then I can pretend too."

Rick became pensive. "After you eat, we can play video games together. You enjoyed playing Smash Brothers with me."

Sandra grinned. "Ok!"

***

Molly pulled into the gravel driveway of their blue ranch-style house, acutely aware of each pop of the stones as they shifted under the weight of her tires. It used to be one of her favorite sounds; either Rick was returning from work, or she was returning and her family was inside. Now it was an alarm clock waking her up to the tragedy that she lived in. At least Sandra would be there, and she could focus on her.

She turned off the car, and a wave of anxiety suddenly hit her, needles in her gut and her heart pounding rapidly in her chest, and she gripped the wheel and took deep breaths. *Get your shit together, Mol,* she thought. *You can do this. Just one thing at a time. One moment at a time. Your daughter's in there with him. You trust him with Sandra. It'll be ok for you.*

Molly exited the car with sudden conviction and headed to the front door, not pausing before it, lest she lose her nerve. The door swung in with enough force that she had to catch it before it hit the closet door behind it.

"Hey Babe. I wasn't sure when you'd be back, so I put a dinner plate together for you. It's in the fridge," Rick said.

"Hey mom!" Sandra shouted.

The two were sitting on the couch in front of the TV, intensely playing a video game.

"H…hey," she replied. She had been so sure that her Rick was gone, but he just called her Babe. He hadn't called her anything but Molly since he woke from his coma. The tile beneath her feet suddenly felt like sand, and she moved into the kitchen and sat.

"I've beaten you twenty-five times in a row. Your insistence on using the same character and strategy is flawed. You need to…switch it up."

"But I *like* Toad," Sandra said.

"Then use a different strategy. I don't know how you're not bored by losing repeatedly," Rick replied.

Now that sounded like dead Rick, Molly thought. But not entirely. Dead Rick wouldn't tell her to 'switch it up', nor would he use the word bored. Dead Rick didn't understand the concept of boredom.

"Rick, are you feeling…?" she was going to say 'ok', but just left the statement there. She dared not allow herself to feel any hope.

"Dad's had a breakthrough, mom," Sandra said, wincing as Rick blasted her character off the board.

"I've made some progress. Sandra made me see things differently," Rick followed.

"Progress," Sandra concluded.

Molly looked down at her hands. They were shaking. This was too good to be true.

"So you see things…differently. But you don't feel any differently?" she asked.

"Correct," Rick said.

**

Molly stormed off into her bedroom, slamming the door behind her, and Sandra glared at Rick.

"Dad!"

"I erred," Rick said.

"Duh. That's the second thing you need to learn. You can't just say everything that pops into your head," Sandra said tersely.

"But it's true. We taught you to always tell the truth."

Sandra groaned. How could she explain something so complicated?

"The truth hurt mom."

"What would you have had me say instead?" he asked.

Sandra thought for a moment. "You could have just said you were working on it. That's the truth too."

"Deflection," Rick said.

"Sure. Yeah. Sometimes the truth hurts, but you have to decide if it's worth it or not. Like, Joanie at school has a mole on her lip. It's brown and really, really gross. It has a hair that comes out of it, and I want to barf every time I look at it. But Joanie's my best friend, so I'm not going to tell her the truth that I think her mole is gross. That wouldn't help my friendship with Joanie, and there's nothing I can do about it anyway."

"I think I understand," Rick said. "I don't know how to fix this," he said, looking toward the bedroom.

Sandra followed his gaze. "I think you need to tell her something she wants to hear, that is also the truth."

"What does she want to hear?" Rick asked.

"I dunno. Maybe that her husband is still in there somewhere?"

Rick nodded.

***

Rick stood in front of the bedroom door, not with apprehension, but in contemplation. He remembered that Molly would not want him to enter without permission, so he knocked softly.

"Molly? Can we talk?" It was as close a facsimile in tone and inflection to a previous incident as he could muster. He waited a moment, and the door opened a crack. Molly walked back to the bed and sat down.

Rick followed, sitting next to her. He studied her posture and her tear-stained face, and it was clear she was in distress. What had he done before in such a situation?

"Hey," he said, reaching out and putting a hand on hers.

"What is this, Rick?" she said with a frown.

"I'm trying. I'm trying to get better. For you and for Sandra."

Molly pulled her hand away. "Why?" she asked with a scowl. "You have no emotions. You don't care."

"But I do care," Rick said.

"Why? I asked you why."

Because this place is familiar. Because you and Sandra are familiar. Because this requires less effort than finding a new place to live. Because Sandra is partially my responsibility. Because I swore an oath to remain with you until death do us part, and society values people that keep their word. Because I would lose assets if we divorced.

The thoughts swirled into Rick's head, one after the other, but none made it to his lips.

"Because I choose to."

***

"Do you desire sex?" Rick asked.

Molly shrugged. "Do you?"

"Yes. My balls are full," he replied.

"I'll think about it," she said, letting her book rest on her chest and staring up at the bedroom ceiling.

Two months had passed since he came to check on her in this bedroom. He'd been back at work for a month, and he'd been sleeping with her for a similar amount of time. While life wasn't the way it had been before his accident, it was a new normal. Rick's 'declaration of choice', as she thought of it, wasn't much, but it was enough to stop her feelings of insecurity, and once they subsided, she began to heal.

And the sex was great. Jen *was* right on that score; having a man that was incapable of moral judgment opened their sex life to every dark and unseemly desire that had ever crossed her mind. She wasn't sure if it was worth trading Rick's humanity for it, but he had become a decent actor, enough for her to momentarily forget that he was…vacant.

Molly's every train of thought still led back to that station, even if the rides were getting longer between stops, and thoughts of sex were frozen out of her mind.

"Dr. Moss, the people at the university, nobody's been able to figure out what's wrong with you. Do *you* still want to know?" she asked, but wasn't sure why she was asking it. She doubted he had a 'want' either way.

"I do," he said.

"Why? You're not capable of curiosity," she pointed out.

"No, but I believe that knowing the reason could lead to a cure, and that's what you want more than anything."

"If there was a cure, you'd seek it?" she asked.

"If that's what you want, yes. I want you and Sandra to be happy."

There it was again, an expressed desire for their well-being. She'd questioned him repeatedly over the last two months, what merited his concern for them? His reply was always the same: "I choose to be concerned." His choice that had initially eased her insecurities had now begun to gnaw at her. What was his motivation? Why *make* that choice? She'd asked him that once, directly. He replied with "why does it matter?" And why did it matter to her? When two people fell in love, did they question the motives behind their commitment? No. But it was driven by a chemical attraction. There was a biological *reason*. Molly figured that's why so many people got divorced. Once that chemical attraction ran its course, the rose-colored glasses came off and the relationship only existed on merit. There was no biological reason with Rick now; he could empty his balls as easily as she could.

"I do want that. Jen made a suggestion a few months ago. I thought it was weird, so I didn't take her up on it, but since the doctors can't give us any answers, I don't think we have anything to lose."

"What was her suggestion?" Rick asked. He turned on his side to look at her, because it implied curiosity.

"She goes to a psychic regularly. She thought she might be able to see something the doctors couldn't."

"There is merit in her suggestion," he said.

Molly propped herself up in surprise and looked at him. "Really?"

Rick nodded. "We're limited by our perceptions. For example, there's many wavelengths of light that exist that we can't see, because our eyes are unable to see them. Yet we know they exist. Perhaps psychics are people who have an enhanced ability to see what the majority can't."

"But psychics have been around for all of human civilization, and they're still dismissed as charlatans. If there was something to it, don't you think science would have caught on by now?" she asked.

Rick shrugged. "We know shorter and longer wavelengths of light exist because we can measure them with tools. If what psychics can sense can't be measured with tools, then science can't prove it exists."

"Like God," she mused.

***

Madame Chandra wasn't what Molly was expecting. More precisely, Molly didn't know she had an expectation until the trio were greeted by a young, athletic-looking blonde woman wearing a Sigma Theta Rho sorority sweatshirt and plain black leggings.

"Jen!" Chandra exclaimed with a smile. "These must be your friends you told me about," she said, leaning on the doorframe to look around Jen at the couple. "Molly and Rick, right?"

"Yes, hi," Molly said with uncertainty.

Chandra gave Molly a mock frown. "You were expecting a gypsy. Most people do. I'm the real deal, though, not a carny. But I do have a Roma headscarf I can put on if it'll make you feel better."

"N…no, it's fine," Molly stammered, her discomfort growing. "I just never believed in this stuff."

"And you still don't, I'm sure," Chandra said. "But you're here, so that means you're desperate, am I right?"

"She is," Rick said stoically.

Molly glared at him.

"Well, come inside, please. I hope to make a believer out of you, but if I don't, I'm getting paid either way, so…" she shrugged, then stood aside allowing them to enter her house.

The trio moved past her, and Molly couldn't find anything odd about the place. It was a normal suburban home, with normal suburban things.

"Head straight back into the living room and make yourselves comfortable. I'll be in in a moment," Chandra said.

Molly and Rick followed Jen into Chandra's living room. Finally, there was something that met Molly's expectations: The room was dimly lit, and a large orange crystal sat on a table in the center. The room was ringed with comfortable leather couches and a single chair, presumably Chandra's. The three sat.

"Jen called me and told me all about Rick's situation," Chandra said from another room. "My specialty is in auras and psychic energy. It's possible I'll be able to figure out what's wrong, or possibly even perform some healing rituals. I've helped people with all kinds of ailments, but you're the first person I've seen that's lost their personality."

"It's not that," Molly replied. "He has no emotions at all."

"Well, let's see what we can do." Chandra walked into the room then, and immediately halted, staring at Rick. "Oh."

No one spoke. A faint ticking from a clock in another room was the only sound.

"Rick, can you stand up, please? Move around the room," Chandra asked.

Rick did as instructed, then sat back down on the couch.

"What is it?" Molly asked.

"I...I don't know," Chandra said uncomfortably. She didn't sit in her chair, rather stood there awkwardly, appearing as if she'd rather be anywhere else in the world.

Molly looked at Jen, and Jen at Chandra.

"What does that mean, you don't know?" Jen asked. "You stopped my migraines last year. You told me I was going to have a run of bad luck in 2018, which I started to, and then you stopped it with your crystal healing. You always have answers for everything."

"It means I don't know," Chandra replied, biting down on her thumb as she continued to stare at Rick.

Molly couldn't contain her emotions any longer, and she stood, taking a step towards Chandra. "Look, lady, you know *something*. There's something wrong with my husband, and no one can tell us what. But it's obvious you know, so spit it the fuck out!"

Molly's aggressive advance broke Chandra out of her confused paralysis, and she took a step back, putting up her hands. "All I know is that what I see in Rick isn't possible, ok? If it's not possible, then I don't know what I'm seeing, so I can't give you an answer. I'm sorry."

Molly's face flushed with anger, and she took another step forward. Jen stood as well, ready to hold Molly back if necessary. Rick watched the whole scene unfold incuriously.

"Is this about money? Just a game to get more? Well, here…" Molly dug around in her purse and pulled out her pocketbook, opened it, and pulled out a fold of twenties. She began throwing them at Chandra one at a time. "...here, take more money. Take all my money! Do you want more? I'll go to the fucking ATM. Just tell me what's wrong with my husband!"

Chandra took another step back, appearing horrified and offended. "I told you, I'm not a fucking charlatan. I take my gift seriously. Take your money. I'm not charging you anything."

Molly clenched her fists and grit her teeth, tears now streaming down her cheeks. Jen held her hands up between them, moving to impose herself physically.

"Chandra, ok, we get it, you don't want to make a guess and be wrong. I know you take this seriously, or else I wouldn't have suggested they see you. But can you please tell us what it looks like to you, even if it's not possible? Mol can't leave here not knowing what you know. It'll tear her up," Jen pleaded.

"Ok, ok. Understand that what I see isn't possible, ok? If it's not possible, it can't be true. It's just how it *appears*."

"So noted," Jen said, then turned to Molly. "You got it? Biiiiig asterisk floating over this."

29

Molly nodded.

"Ok," Chandra said, then took a deep breath. "It appears to me that Rick doesn't have a soul."

The room went silent again. Jen broke it.

"Say what now?"

"It looks like he doesn't have a soul," Chandra repeated, sitting down in her chair.

"What, like a zombie or vampire or something?" Jen asked.

"Those aren't real," Chandra hissed.

"Why…why isn't that possible?" Molly asked, sitting back on the couch.

"Because when the soul departs the body, the body dies," Chandra answered.

"What about near-death experiences?" Jen asked.

"When that happens, the soul begins to depart, but the body heals before the process is completed," Chandra answered, then sat in her chair. "There's no way you can stuff a soul back into a body after it separates, and no way for a body to live independently without a soul."

"What does he look like to you, Chandra?" Jen asked, returning to her couch. "Is there no aura?"

"Not quite. He has a dim aura, like a tree. The spirit and the soul are different things. All life has spirit as a consequence of being alive."

"So he is alive," Molly stated.

"Yes. Clearly," Chandra said.

"Perhaps you simply can't see my aura," Rick stated.

Everyone turned to Rick, who until that point had been as inanimate as the couch.

"Humans can't see into the infrared or ultraviolet spectrums. Maybe my soul aura transformed after the accident into something you can't see?" he continued.

Chandra shook her head. "That doesn't make any sense. You can't equate physical senses to the supernatural senses."

"Why not?" Rick asked.

Molly interrupted. "No, she's right, Rick. Everything she's saying makes sense. There was something missing when you woke up from the coma. I've been saying that I'm living with your corpse."

Jen nodded and looked at Rick. "She has."

"I believe you. And whether or not you think it's possible, I believe my husband has no soul," Molly said. "If a tree can live without a soul, so can he."

"But, trees weren't made to have souls," Chandra protested, but the matter was concluded. "What did they do to him in the hospital?"

Molly sighed. "Dr. Moss, an ER doctor at the university hospital, invented a new life-support prototype that, and these are his words, hold the chakras open until the body heals. I looked up chakras on the internet…"

"What?" Chandra exclaimed, jumping up from her chair. "Were Rick's chakras closed already when they put him in that machine?"

Molly appeared stunned. "I…How should I know?"

***

No one spoke on the ride home, and now Rick and Molly sat across from each other in silence at the kitchen table. Chandra had explained to them that when the body dies, the chakras close from the feet up, essentially squeezing the soul out the top of the head like toothpaste out of the tube. So long as the soul was paired with the body, chakras could reopen, but if they had all closed, if Rick's soul had departed, then he should be dead. Chandra said it was like turning off the lights when you left the house. Except Dr. Moss figured out how to turn the lights back on when no one was home. Rick was soulless.

Molly looked up at him as he stared vacantly at the wood grain of the table. There was nothing in there; just a machine running a biological program of action and reaction. Rick was dead and his body should be dead. Its presence at her table was an insult to Rick's memory, an affront to decency, a perversion of nature. She didn't owe it anything, and she couldn't live like this anymore.

"I want a divorce," Molly said flatly.

"Why?" Rick asked. "Have I offended you in some way?"

"Because my Rick is dead. You're nothing more than an animated corpse."

"Possibly. But you've seemed happy the last two months. I've been trying very hard to be more normal."

"Have I really, Rick? It was different when I convinced myself you were just profoundly impaired. But you're not impaired, Rick. You're a walking bag of meat with my husband's memories. Nothing more. A tree made of meat."

"People value trees. They provide shade. They have aesthetic value. They suck carbon from the air."

"And you add carbon to it for no reason. You should be dead. I need to move on. Sandra and I both need to move on," Molly said. She looked into Rick's unfeeling eyes, and she herself felt nothing.

"Sandra and I have a good relationship. She needs a father. I provide 63.5% of the household income."

Why was he fighting her on this, Molly wondered? He didn't care because he didn't have the capacity to care. He had no emotional attachment.

"Let me be as clear as possible, Rick. Tonight, you're sleeping on the couch. Tomorrow, I'm taking Sandra to school, then going to work. When I come home, you'll be gone. I never want to see you again. Not from ten feet away, not from a thousand yards away. I won't have your presence fucking with Sandra's heart. I don't care where you go. I don't care what you do. My husband died three months ago."

***

Mr. Mossman the tree stood sentinel in the woods behind Rick's house, its wide, meandering branches casting shade so thick onto the ground that the only things that could grow beneath it were mushrooms and moss. That's why Sandra chose the name. She and Rick would play in these woods, so it was a familiar place for Rick to go to think. Sandra would be home soon, and he wasn't sure if he should be there when she arrived.

Rick sat between two roots, paying no mind to a family of mushrooms that he squashed beneath him. That would have bothered him in the past, he knew. The dirt, the mush, the mess. It would have revolted him. He would have worried about stains and bugs. But there was nothing off-putting about it now. Just matter against matter. He leaned back against the old oak and felt the bark pressing into his back. He closed his eyes.

Rick wished to stay, but Molly was clear that he should go. It made sense to ask Sandra what her wishes were, as a tiebreaker, yet he knew she would want him to stay. That would put him into direct conflict with Molly. Did Sandra deserve a father more than Molly deserved to grieve?

Rick felt something on his foot and opened his eyes to find a squirrel perched there. The scent of crushed mushrooms must have lured it, Rick figured. He had heard of tame squirrels. He and Sandra watched a few videos of them on YouTube. Yet this squirrel was wild, and humans were dangerous. Rick watched the squirrel hop to his other foot. It stood up and sniffed the air, then moved down his leg right onto his lap.

The squirrel hopped about his lap and legs for a quarter hour, investigating his pants and shoes, sniffing the air, trying to find the mushrooms that Rick was sitting upon. It hopped down between his legs, then jammed his arrow-shaped head as far under Rick's crotch as he could. It tickled, but Rick continued to watch impassively. The squirrel began to dig, attempting to open a gap beneath him that would liberate the mushrooms. As the gap grew wider, it was able to insert more of its furry body into the space. Rick could feel the squirrel's body heat pressing against him. Still not finding the mushrooms, it sat up and took in the entirety of the scene, eventually meeting Rick's gaze. Startled, it jumped a foot in the air, its furry tail swinging about wildly, and scampered away.

Rick understood. Something intangibly human was missing, and even with his human scent, without that intangible something, to the squirrel, Rick was as inanimate as the tree he was leaning against. He knew he had to go. It was…what word would he have used before the accident? A kindness? Sandra could get a new father, one that had feelings, but Molly would never be free of her grief if he stayed. The only matter for him to decide was how he would depart. Would a goodbye be beneficial or detrimental to Sandra?

As the school bus pulled up in front of the house, his mind began to parse the data, impassively, objectively, attempting to make the most humane decision he could.

T.S. DeBrosse

LIFE AND DEPTH

Marcella savored the caress of the sun on her cheeks, the salty breeze tousling her hair as it swept in from the vast expanse of the Atlantic. It would be a grueling two month mission and the sailors had cooked up a deep sea fish for fun. The fish wasn't reported, of course–who knew if it was a recognized species. The strange sea creature had attached itself to the submarine. After the submarine had surfaced, the fish was extracted during cleaning. It had a putrid smell, black, oily skin, deep gill grooves, and tiny ear buds–a grotesque amalgamation. Marcella ate it with lime. It was salty with a twang, and grittier than expected. Afterwards, her breath smelled of dill pickles.

She felt it her duty to eat it as a way of demonstrating her mettle to the other sailors before heading into the ocean for a government research expedition. Marcella's area of study involved hydrothermal vents and the genesis of life. She was to board a Navy submarine, and the blending of service members and scholarly postdocs induced palpable trepidation. Rules barring women from crewing subs had only just been lifted, and Marcella was keen to fit in.

A new guy had been added to the mission last minute. Below deck, he held his hand out to Marcella. "Hello, my name is Imrich." He had close-cropped, sand-colored hair and a bit of an accent which she fancied.

"I'm Marcella. Where are you from?" She hoped it wasn't rude to ask. Then she recognized his US Navy crewmen uniform and instantly felt foolish. "I mean, where is your *accent* from?" Her cheeks flushed.

"My accent is from the Czech Republic. I am a non-citizen, but I have my green card." He addressed the inquiry with poise, unfazed, and grinned, as though answering the same question over and over again was okay.

Ah! Someone interesting to connect with. She flashed him a smile. "My grandparents were from Czechoslovakia, now in the spot that's Slovakia. But I know there's shared history. I don't know much about the region, but would love to learn more." And she meant it. Marcella ached to know more about her ancestral homeland. Her parents and grandparents were gone, and her own sense of identity was in flux.

Marcella tucked a loose strand of hair behind her ear, felt the tender bruise on her neck, and then brought the hair forward again to cover it with a shaky hand.

"Oh?" he said, and his eyes twinkled. "I can teach you many things. But I do like to talk, so tell me off when you've had enough." He must not have seen the bruise. Marcella decided then that she liked him.

Marcella made her way into her sleeping quarters, where the dim glow of the overhead lamps bathed the simple, narrow bunks. A lump of blankets stirred on the top bunk. It was Sun-Young Shin, an engineering postdoc who was tough as nails and had been her steadfast companion during orientation. They'd boarded the *Porbeagle* together. Sun-Young held her hand out from the blanket.

"I traded for a bag of trail mix." Sun-Young shook the bag. "Want some?"

"Yes, definitely. Did you eat that weird deep sea fish? I keep burping up this dill taste." It was nauseating, and Marcella allowed her saliva to pool in her mouth then drank it down, only for the distinct dill taste of the black, oily fish to bubble up again in the back of her throat.

"Thank God I did not try that nasty fish. I hope the sub doesn't stink from it. Can you imagine? Everyone burping it up? No ventilation? Please," she shook the bag again. "Good on you for being adventurous, I think. But that was so gross. Eat all the cranberries. They're infused with orange flavor so you'll burp up citrus."

Marcella obliged, plucking the cranberries from the mix and popping them into her mouth. Afterwards, she unpacked her seabag, setting her four folded uniforms aside to retrieve a small print of her house. Someone had sketched it for her years ago—with its wrap-around porch and mismatched shutters. It was the house she grew up in, once belonging to her grandparents. Now it was hers, but it didn't feel like it. The energy felt wrong, like recent memories wouldn't anchor. Marcella hung the print beside her bed, the dim overhead lights barely illuminating it. She smoothed her blanket down. It felt cool against her clammy hand. She'd broken out into a sweat. The submarine already felt claustrophobic. Marcella had trained for the long haul and was determined to ride out the expedition smoothly, as her career depended on it.

The lights flickered and Marcella felt a drop. The walls creaked. Mechanical sounds pounded metal like sacrificial drumming.

Down.

Down.

Down.

Beyond the steel hull the ocean teemed with life, its mysteries hidden in the depths, and she focused on that expansiveness to ground herself. Marcella shivered—an intrusive thought, being crushed from the pressure, flashed in her mind and her death was instant. Had it happened just now? No. Marcella took a deep breath, but then coughed up more of the acrid fish.

"Please relax," said Sun-Young, still under her blankets. "I can feel the stress emanating from your body."

"You're the one hiding under a blanket."

"Yeah, well when I emerge, the sub will seem roomy." Sun-Young threw off her blankets and stretched.

"Here we go," said Marcella with a nervous laugh. She burped and excused herself to find the rest of her team.

***

Two weeks into the research expedition and the submarine combed the depths along the Mid-Atlantic Ridge. First crew made their way to breakfast after drills. The narrow corridors meant that Marcella had to pin her body against the wall any time a sailor passed from the other direction. There were one-hundred-and-five sailors and civilians, and Marcella's walks were frequently punctuated by this inconvenience.

Marcella rounded the corner—she could see her destination, center-left and third booth in—and yet she stepped back into the kitchen recess. She spent a lot of her mornings there, waiting patiently for the crew to thin out. At last, she stepped out from the kitchen, then froze as the sub groaned, silencing everyone for a spell.

Marcella, eyes wide, walked down the aisle and carefully eased herself into the booth, where three guys sat across from Sun-Young, all of their faces turning to the wall behind the kitchen, the source of the mechanical din. The shortest of the three men peeled his eyes off the wall and looked at Marcella and Sun-Young.

"Well thank God I have a good life insurance policy," he quipped.

"I always thought that shit was a morbid racket," said Sun-Young, leaning back.

"Not if you have someone waiting for you back home."

Sun-Young rolled her eyes. "You do you."

The submarine groaned again, this time from above. It was loud—too loud, and everyone dropped down. The seconds ticked.

Everyone eased upright again. Marcella looked around. "Where's Declan? I'm sure they're on it. Do you need to head out, Sun-Young?"

"I'm fine. They got people on it, for sure," said Sun-Young.

"I have a fiance back home. His name is Hugo," began Marcella. *Why am I telling them this?* "We live right outside Philadelphia. We're um, well, I'm hoping to call it off after this expedition. Sorry, we were talking about life insurance? Significant others? I'm not gonna lie, that groaning sound is scaring the shit out of me." She shrugged, but her throat tightened like the air was being squeezed out of her.

"You're calling it off after you get home? Should have ended the relationship before you left, don't you think?" said the taller man.

"Yes, yes," she waved him off.

Imrich appeared beside Marcella. He placed his plate on the table and then scooted in beside her.

"Everyone okay?" he asked.

Marcella took a deep breath, blinked, and registered for a second the lightness of Imrich's presence. *How peculiar.*

"Sun-Young, they're going to need you–" began Imrich.

"Goddamnit, can't I just enjoy my oatmeal?" Sun-Young slammed her fist on the table. "It's bananas and cream. They never have bananas and cream!" Her scowl turned to a fierce smile and she spooned up her oatmeal.

The silence that followed amplified Sun Young's chewing, and when that was over, the usual hum of machinery and the steady thrum of the engine seemed distant, drowned out by the palpable tension. Everyone was acutely aware of the immense weight of the ocean pressing down on their fragile vessel.

"Each day the universe reveals more of herself," said Imrich, and the other men looked at him like they'd seen a ghost.

Sun-Young raised an eyebrow.

No one liked Imrich, but that didn't matter to Marcella. She liked him a lot, liked the heat of his body, the bounce of his voice, the thoughtful attention he paid her.

Sun-Young clapped her hands together. "Okay! Well everyone, on that note, I'm out." Sun-Young lifted her plate and waited for Marcella and Imrich to move out of the booth, then scooted around them to make her way to the sink.

"I should probably head out too." Marcella felt a bubble rise in her throat and then burped. "Excuse me. I'm due on sonar. We're updating the map before we attempt the submersible."

"We shouldn't go any deeper," cautioned Imrich. "Our vessel can't get much closer to the heart."

Marcella stood for a spell, wavering under his influence. "Of course we can." She winked.

* * *

"I swear I'll never eat a pickle again, or anything fermented," Marcella whispered to Imrich as they passed through the corridor after the crew meeting. They were nearing the end of the mission and her mysterious symptoms hadn't let up. The dill taste, the constant, churning bile. The feeling of deep, raw fissures in her tonsils. The slight lump on the back of her neck. "They say my lymph nodes feel fine, but I seriously question that."

Imrich lowered his brow and stared at her. "Today let's sit one row up from our regular spot."

"One row up?" Marcella laughed.

"It will break up the monotony and cultivate perspective." Imrich turned from her, his hand finding hers, then pushed through the sea of sailors, who moved both towards them and away. Imrich was a strong hull, and the sea parted before him. Marcella traveled down the middle of the narrow corridor—a first. Imrich eased into a booth, one row up from their usual hang, and Marcella slipped in across from him. She glanced around and took note of the different angles, the rectangular painting of the swordfish no longer stretched, the small recess of the kitchen now invisible to the eye.

"I think you should try another of my elixirs," said Imrich in a flat tone.

"Imrich!" she leaned in closer to him. "It makes me feel strange."

"Strange, but better." He reached across the table and tucked her hair behind her ear.

She stared at him, her smile a half moon, and his other hand came up behind her head, tipping her forward slightly, and he kissed her.

"I've got my mortar and pestle at the ready." Imrich leaned back in his chair, studying her.

"I'm sure you do," said Marcella. She winced at the memory of flakes of wormwood catching in the back of her throat.

"This ailment of yours," continued Imrich. "It could be the pressure. Pressure does weird things to a body," he said. "Anxiety, too." He pulled his rabbit's foot from his back pocket and started rolling it between his hands.

"I've got anxiety about my reflux. And about that deep sea fish, a totally unnatural diet for us terrestrial mammals, by the way." Her eyes honed in on the rabbit's foot. He often carried it with him. It wasn't all fur. The end had two inches of exposed bone that had been whittled down.

"Ah, caught in a loop," he said with a smile.

Marcella felt her throat burn. "I'm almost out of here. I just have to hold off on any further medical attention until we're off the sub. I can't be flagged as unable to withstand living on a submarine."

"Mind's bouncing like a rabbit." Imrich held his rabbit's foot up, grinned.

"On the bright side–with the data I'm seeing–I'm going to explore the idea of how geochemistry and biochemistry might align. We're witnessing the creation of a sort of primitive enzyme along the vent. And there's Sun-Young!" Marcella jumped up from the table, but Imrich said, "Wait!"

She flinched. Imrich held his hands up in surrender. "Give me a moment more. Do you see?" He shook the rabbit's foot.

Marcella froze, half-certain he was joking. "Yes, I see the rabbit's foot." She crossed her arms. "So is it luck I need, Imrich? The last bastion of good health, luck and prayer. And the rabbit's foot would get me published, too."

"No, I've been grinding the bone at the end." Imrich turned the rabbit foot over and Marcella nodded. She saw more than she'd meant. "Meditative, for me," he continued.

"That's too macabre." Marcella frowned. "But meditation, sure. I could try that. I have been awfully excitable, between my health and my research."

"Yes, of course. Sorry." Imrich tucked the rabbit's foot back into his pocket. "It's said that stress and worry impede the immune system, that the inflammation caused by unchecked disease, virus, and bacteria repopulates and manifests as physical pain."

"Is this supposed to make me feel better?" A light flickered. Marcella's eyes darted to the wall, but quickly found their way back to Imrich.

"You are weak—"

Marcella raised an eyebrow to him, daring him.

"Ask yourself, why am I weak? Could it be the stress, the worry? Your immune system is misfiring. Is it a virus, Marcella? Something grows and this angry inflammation festers. Ah, to get to the root of the problem... that's...?" Imrich shrugged. "If you figure it out, let me know. But if you won't take my elixir, meditation might help you to understand." He stared at her with intense green eyes, and Marcella cocked her head to the side, her mind fumbling to process his musings. Something clicked. What was it, pushing against her brain just now?

Marcella glanced down at her hands, which she'd been drumming on the table, then returned her gaze to his face. He wore an open expression. "We could all do to re-center ourselves." Marcella took a deep breath.

"What centers a person? Where is that?"

Marcella laughed, unsure how to respond. Her head? Her heart? Or was it a sense of belonging? The idea struck her and her stomach flipped. If she could feel a void, an unmet need, and the ache was caused by a longing, then the antidote might be to find the place she belonged.

"I think you'll find your way home, Marcella."
Imrich folded his hands together on the table and smiled.

Marcella returned a soft smile, stupefied, and then
stood up. A dizziness swept over her. And then the lights
went out.

A groaning sound.

Shouting.

Metal on metal snapping.

Marcella was thrown to the side, knocked to the
floor. She rose, stumbled forward, caught her balance, and
then extended her arms, groping at the blackness. The
dark made her one with the depths of the ocean, void of
light, sound muffled. And there she floated for a while, in-
between her body and the black expanse. She reached out
and made contact with a wall—no, it was someone, and her
senses coalesced. But then they weren't anymore. The
body had pulled away. Which way did it go? To the
engine? Where did the system failure originate?

She smelled smoke. It was a thick, noxious smoke
that immediately seized up her lungs, now heavy rocks
pressing against her heart. Her airways constricted. Her
eyes burned.

Marcella assumed she'd drop to the ground to avoid the smoke, let it snake around her and drag her into oblivion. But instead her legs carried her forward, propelled by the instinct to live, despite it all. She turned a corner, and then remembered the emergency breaker by the kitchen. She pushed back towards the tide of bodies and slipped into the recess. Here, she could manually override the system by shutting down the breakers, then recalibrate the power distribution. She'd hugged this corner so many times, pressing against the wall, making room for others to pass, sometimes stepping back into the kitchen–*drop down, knee level*–there! She groped at the panel, flipping every switch to off, then felt around for a button, any button. She felt one, pressed it–nothing. She felt another, pressed it, then the emergency lights went on, soft electric blue, buzzing defiantly in the gloom. But there was no time to take stock of the illumination, and she ran, sensing that behind her, a sea of bodies pressed dangerously forward, clawing, climbing.

She moved quickly now through the maze of tight corridors. At the end of a hallway, she could see lit helmets and arms that beckoned forward. She ran to those arms now, squeezed through as the door became jammed, and got to the other side, where open fresh air enveloped her. Sun-Young appeared and grabbed her by the shoulder. "With me," she said, and Marcella was pulled forward, led to a control room, mayday calls piercing the chaos, and left there.

Voices in the dark, broken fragments of narrative, fell on her ears: "There's a leak–"

"--electrical fire!"

"...Compartment sealed..."

"They're trapped!"

Marcella closed her eyes but the evacuation lights were burned into her retinas, a glow she couldn't escape, flitting wildly across her universe like mischievous fae.

An oxygen masked was shoved into her hands, and she turned it over, grasping at its strings and coils, eventually securing it to her face.

The minutes ticked by, her breathing slowed, and then a bright light filled the cabin. Marcella winced, then scrambled to her feet.

A few stray hollers followed by disembodied responses, full-bellied and authoritative.

Jubilation. Full power was restored.

Sun-Young arrived back at the control room and removed the helmet of her survival suit, sweat streaming down her face. "We're stable, thank God! We're okay. We're going to be okay." She ran her hands through her hair, cursing as she caught her breath. "Distress signal went through too so we're initiating a controlled ascent."

"So now we *have* to seize the day," said Marcella, finding her voice. She let her oxygen mask fall to the floor and hugged Sun-Young.

"So you'll kick that fiancé to the curb? Damn if I don't find someone and buy life insurance," Sun-Young laughed.

Marcella laughed too, her body still shaking from the shock of survival. "Soon, yes! Soon. 'Nač stahovat kalhoty, když brod je ještě daleko?' Czech proverb. It means, 'Why put your pants down while the ford is still far away?' Imrich taught it to me."

"Right," said Sun-Young. "Funny guy."

Marcella smiled. "It means, 'Everything in due time.'"

* * *

Up.
Up.
Up.

The pressure lifted.

Marcella sat in a camping chair by the firepit, her head swimming. The pregnancy test read "positive," despite two negative tests prior to boarding the sub two months ago. Last night, she dreamt of the deep sea fish she'd eaten. It grew inside her, the black oil of its flesh splattering all over her womb, infecting her like a cancer, and it grinned all the while like a sly fox.

Tonight, Hugo had thrown her a return party, but it consisted of a lot of faces she'd never met.

Hugo slumped in the camping chair beside Marcella. "You look miserable, knock it off. Hey, you have to meet Chandra! She's wild. She's dating Anthony." He measured his words with hands sweeping across the sky, "Call her, Lady Chandra. No, Madam Chandra!" Hugo smiled and ran his hands through the shaved stubble on his head, waiting for a response.

"Cool," she said at last. Marcella wished he'd never thrown a party. She had to find the right time to call it off with him, and he made it hard. *Seize the day.* She turned to him, and it felt like the earth beneath her tilted, like she was still bobbing in the ocean with Imrich and Sun-Young. "Do you ever feel like something is missing? Like, your roots are in the wrong soil?" She thought of Imrich's face now, his green, half-lidded eyes, his thumb massaging the tip of the rabbit bone.

Hugo let out a forced laugh, then cleared his throat. "Nope, can't say I have." He paused, agitated. "So what, do people get all philosophical on the submarine or something? It's got to be boring as hell. Except for almost-dying. I seriously need more details!"

Tony and Dillon began to sway near the fire, voices rising in a rustic sea shanty. It blended with the drum and bass reverberating from the speakers, pressuring the singers to increase the tempo. Hugo joined in before Marcella could answer.

"To Marcella!" Everyone was smacking together their red solo cups, beer sloshing over the sides, and Marcella felt like she might puke.

"Excuse me," said Marcella, rising from her seat. She turned to make her way to the back shed, a gravity pulling her there as the drum and bass beat with her heart. She bumped into a young woman wearing a Sigma Theta Rho sorority sweatshirt and black leggings.

"Hi! We haven't met yet. I'm Chandra," Chandra extended her hand.

"Yes, hey, I'm Marcella," she said, shaking the woman's hand. "Thanks for coming."

Chandra's expression changed to one of concern, and she didn't let go of Marcella's hand. "Are you feeling okay?"

"You know, I'm actually not," said Marcella, her eyes darting to the shed. She needed to get in there.

"You miss being out in the ocean. I see the dark blue water all around you."

Marcella was growing impatient. "Yes, yes."

"There's something following you." Chandra's brows furrowed. "Forgive me. I read energies, and you've got a separate one attached to your back. May I...? May I have a look? Can you turn?"

Marcella yanked her hand back from Chandra. "I need to go now." She turned and walked towards the shed. Something was in there, aching to be found. She could feel Chandra's eyes on her back, but even more than that, she could feel herself separate from her body, her consciousness buzzing outside the boundaries of her frame. Marcella tried to focus on the leaves of the cherry blossom tree beside the shed, but her head shot to the knobby trunk instead: it was dying. This wasn't native soil.

Her vision blurred, and she looked up, basking her face in the moonlight as her hand reached out to grab the shed door. Her foot crunched the twigs of a fallen bird nest, just as the wind registered on her cheek. Each sensation amplified and swelled within her, crossing through her and finally extending beyond the boundaries of her flesh.

Marcella opened the door. A figure lurked in the corner, its long legs bent at the knees to keep its head from touching the rafters. It appeared to be a wild dog, standing upright with fox ears and curled lips. But the face was all wrong, waxy black where there should be fur, neck slitted and trembling like gills struggling in open air.

Marcella wavered in the doorway, then took a step towards it. "You."

The creature turned from her and knelt. Its claws pulled back the rotten floor board.

Marcella took another step towards the creature, then another, and another, and the two were one, her hands now clawed appendages, and she dug into the earth until her nail beds bled. Moonlight leaked in from a grimy window. She heaved and her stomach flipped, the stench of dill mixing with bile as it sloshed up her throat. Still she dug, instinctively, like some other sense had been awakened, honing in on meat. At last she reached a grouping of large stones under the floorboard. She pulled one from the ground, brushing the dirt from it, and recognized the name etched into it, Bratislava. Her grandmother was from Bratislava, Slovakia. Marcella wiped her mouth on her sleeve: bile, dirt, and blood. Had her grandmother buried this? Then Hugo barged into the shed.

"Can you find the survey to our house? Carrie asked if it was haunted and I think the area by the fence… Hey, bitch, look at me while I'm talking to you. What are you doing?" He stood in the door frame and creased his brow.

Marcella tried to steady her breathing. She could feel the bruise resurface on her neck, the one he'd left there before deployment—or was it the gills of the creature, struggling to breathe?

"Hey, Marcella!"

Marcella stood up, gripping the stone, and then threw it at him, striking his shoulder. He stepped back in astonishment.

"What the fuck?"

Marcella lunged at him, dipping low to seize the stone once more and then springing up to crack it on top of his head. Hugo stumbled, disoriented, and then another crack landed and he fell to the ground, blood gushing from the gash.

Marcella's vision became focused again and she could see from her own eyes and she could feel the cold stone in her hot hand. Marcella stumbled out of the shed and yelled, "Help Hugo!"

She dashed to the firepit and grabbed her pocketbook from the seat of a camping chair, still cradling her large stone. She glanced at it—the etchings were gone. Had she picked up the wrong stone? A few of Hugo's friends stared bewildered at her, while others were running over to the shed.

Marcella sprinted to her car. She moved as though in a dream, layered meaning pressing down on her like a weighted blanket. Then there was clarity: She would take a flight to give birth in Slovakia.

J.D. Marshall

Brain Box

A ray of sunlight pierced the pink drapes and gave Catalina a headache, which was exacerbated by the smell of bleach. With a movement of her eyeballs, she commanded her wheelchair to back away from the light. Soon she was sitting next to Old Moss, who had grown agitated playing a game, his fingers jamming the controller. He spoke in a low, gruff tone, while his wife shushed him. "That NPC isn't supposed to attack the gunman."

Catalina smiled politely and moved her wheelchair to the far side of the room. Moss used to be an accomplished doctor, but now that his brain was addled, he'd become a patient.

"And THAT NPC isn't supposed to pick up a shotgun and point it at me!" he yelled, throwing his controller to the ground. Catalina sighed, then aligned herself with a different monitor. In seconds, a signal streamed into her visual and auditory cortexes, entertainment taking place entirely in her brain, drowning out the antics of the other residents.

An orchestra played the Dawn of Freedom, a sentimental anthem of the new age. The words "Liberation Day" came into view, written in an ornate script. In the background, there was a visual of the U.S. Capitol Building, and then a cut to the House of Representatives. A majority of the members were clapping and cheering, while a smaller group was abandoning the room.

A smooth voice over came on. "Today is Liberation Day, the dawn of freedom. After decades of gridlock and a fractured nation, a brave coalition on the right and left decided to give power back to the people. They voted to dissolve the federal government. Soon thereafter, all state and local governments were also disbanded. Finally, the free market was allowed to flourish. Now we live in a liberated society, where all goods and services are available to you through trusted companies."

"Catalina," said a voice from far away. Catalina switched off the program and slowly returned her attention to the pink room. A nurse was smiling and bending down close to her face. "Catalina, you have a visitor."

The nurse stepped aside, and a tall man in a tailored suit stood before her, his hands folded in front of him. "Good evening, Catalina." Vernon smiled, showing his dimples. "I'm sorry to disturb you, but we have some things to discuss."

Even though she was paralyzed, Catalina could produce speech by thinking words in her mind, generating a neural pattern that was linked to software. It was easy to make words come out; the difficult thing was preventing stray thoughts from being accidentally spoken. "Good to see you, Vern. Been a few years."

"Yes, eleven years, for which I do apologize. Can we speak in private?"

Catalina moved her wheelchair slowly forward. Her eyeballs were sore. "The ping-pong room." They were soon sitting across from each other at a ping-pong table.

"So what's this all about?" Catalina's synthetic voice sounded eerily similar to her former natural voice.

"I will answer that question. But first allow me to compliment you. Your control of your assistive technology is flawless."

"Vern, are you buttering me up for something?"

"Never could get anything past you, Catalina. I'll cut to the chase. Bright Future has made a breakthrough in the field of assistive technology."

"Better ping-pong rackets?"

"Of a sort. The goal is to surgically transfer human consciousness into a synthetic body."

Catalina paused. "And you need a guinea pig. Vern, my brain is all I have left."

"Hear me out. The procedure involves copying every neuron in your brain. One by one, each neuron is replaced with a synthetic neuron. The surgery is very precise, performed with robotic tools and algorithms. When it's done, you will have gained possible immortality."

"But if it doesn't work, I'm a vegetable or dead."

Vernon reached in the pocket of his suit and pulled out a white mouse, placing it on the table. The mouse sniffed around and scuttled under the net towards Catalina. "You see Catalina, Eve did just fine. She was the first surgery, followed by another five hundred mice, two hundred pigs, and fifty chimpanzees. So far, over ninety-nine percent success rate."

Eve came over to Catalina's hand resting on her wheelchair, and sniffed it. "How do I know this is synthetic?"

Vernon stood and came over. "Allow me to demonstrate." Vernon took a piece of skin on Eve and peeled it back, revealing a milky tangle of wires. "A marvel of science. Of course, we couldn't resist giving her some enhancements." Vernon replaced the flap of skin, and it reintegrated seamlessly into the mouse's back.

To Catalina's horror, Vernon grabbed the mouse and tossed it to the ceiling. The mouse spun in the air like a swimmer executing a dive, and as she hit the ceiling, she caught the plaster with her claws. As if nothing had happened, Eve scuttled across the ceiling to the light fixture and began sniffing it.

Catalina rolled her chair to the window. "Impressive. But what happened to the one percent of test subjects who failed the surgery?"

"Well, there were some unpleasant results. But in every case of failure, there was a pre-existing weakness in the brain."

"You see the thing about that… I've been having memory problems ever since the accident," said Catalina.

Vernon leaned in. "I'm very sorry to hear that."

"Some memories are hazy, others have pieces missing. Many are just not there." Catalina paused. "Vern, how did Isaac die?"

Vernon furrowed his brow. "I'm afraid we've had this conversation on many occasions, Catalina. For some reason, you do not retain the information. Perhaps your brain cannot accept the information. But every time we have this conversation, it is very painful."

Catalina digested this, and searched her memory for the prior conversations, but could not find any. "Then tell me about something else. How did you and I meet?"

"Ah," said Vernon, his face relaxing. "I prefer that story. Do you remember the Zlocin family?"

Catalina closed her eyes. "I was a little girl, waking up before dawn. We played a game inside a warehouse full of crates and boxes. The teacher would walk around with a flag on his belt. We would sneak around, trying to take the flag. If he caught you, you were eliminated. But if you took the flag without him noticing, you could have extra food that day."

Vernon nodded. "Yes, you remember your training. Then when you were fourteen, you broke into a satellite office owned by Bright Future. You were trying to steal the design for an ultra-efficient solar panel. We caught you on the way out and offered you more money than the Zlocin family was paying. You accepted, and that's how you became an operative at Bright Future."

"How did I get caught?"

"Funny you should ask that. It wasn't your fault, really. It was your partner, who we detected poking around in our data. You never would've been caught if it wasn't for Godfrey."

At hearing the name Godfrey, Catalina felt a burning in the pit of her stomach. "Who's Godfrey?"

"All will be revealed in time. Let us return to the offer I came to discuss. Allow me to sweeten the pot. If you undergo this surgery, you will have complete access to every memory you have ever encoded. And that's not all. Natural Providence is also engaged in neurological research. We believe that they have preserved Isaac's brain."

"I'm in."

* * *

Catalina was laying on an operating table, holding Vernon's hand. She could feel the anesthesia closing in on her consciousness, her vision contracting to a pinpoint. Then she was swimming in an ocean of darkness, out of time and space. There was a beacon of light, and her head split with pain as the light expanded into a blazing star.

She was awake, laying on the table, a robotic arm whirring over her skull. The left side of her body was numb and she tasted sulfur.

"We have a hemorrhage. She's having a brain stem stroke," said a voice.

Catalina's headache began to roar, the pain crashing through her like a waterfall, the universe bulging and about to explode. Then she was back in the ocean of darkness.

Catalina opened her eyes. At first, she thought she was looking through thermal imaging goggles, but when she reached up to her face, it was bare. She was in a room with a patchwork of blue shapes denoting walls and furniture. Greenish-yellow footprints led in and out of the doorway. Orange fingerprints speckled the screen of a machine next to her.

Catalina closed her eyes now and listened. Sound was more granular than she had ever heard. There was a squeak of a wheel and the thrum of an MRI machine. She reached farther out to a hushed conversation and heard "flush out any software vulnerabilities."

Footsteps padded towards her room, and someone knocked softly on the door. "Come in, Vern," she said.

The door swung open and Vernon walked in wearing his usual three-piece suit. Through her thermal vision, she could see the man standing in front of her was not glowing red and orange as expected, but rather was a cool patchwork of blue streaked with bright lines about the width of wires. "Vern, did you have the operation too?"

"Good morning, Catalina. I see you are already making use of your new abilities. How are you feeling?"

Catalina sat up in bed. "I feel incredible. But you didn't answer my question."

71

Vernon clasped his hands in front of him. "I hope you will forgive me for keeping this from you all those years, but Bright Future had to take extraordinary measures to keep its technology from falling into the wrong hands. In answer to your question, no, I did not have the operation done." Vernon paused. "I have always been a synthetic."

Hours later, they were in a room with three tanks full of red liquid and human bodies inside. Catalina walked to the center tank and put her hand on the glass. There was Isaac's muscular body floating in the center. "Oh my God, it looks just like him." Catalina moved her face closer to the glass. She felt that tears should come, but they did not.

Vernon turned away. "The tank contains just the outer layer of the synthetic body. The rest of him is being assembled in a Bright Future factory. Soon the only missing piece will be the brain."

Catalina gritted her teeth. "I'm gonna get what Godfrey stole from me."

They continued into another room full of laboratory equipment. Catalina could hardly believe what she saw standing in the center of the room on a raised dais. It was a replica of her wearing a black suit.

"You're cloning me now?"

"Not at all. She is merely a robotic tool, capable of many forms and functions. With a certain level of artificial intelligence, of course. But she has no consciousness per se. You are a hundred percent in control."

Catalina circled the replica warily. "How does it work?"

"Ah. For that, you will need a software update." Vernon tapped his arm. "Brace yourself. This is going to feel a little strange."

Catalina felt her mind filling up with long strings of computer code and images of possible configurations for her robot replica. Learning so much new information in a few seconds was intoxicating. Catalina crouched down in ecstasy. "More updates."

* * *

A translucent shape shot across the sky, as quiet as the breeze. Catalina's robot replica was on her back, fashioned into a jetpack that propelled her through the air, the wind cascading over her skin. She was invisible thanks to her quantum cloaking device, which camouflaged her on every point of the electromagnetic spectrum.

In the distance, a mountain emerged, shaped like a thumb poking the sky. The air grew foul and hazy with pollution, and Catalina could just make out the iron dome in the valley below. Switching to her infrared vision, she saw the faint blue outline of a tiny helicopter, the first security drone of Natural Providence. She slowed down to match the speed of the wind around her and glided past the drone, emitting no detectable energy.

She passed a few more, and then came to an outer perimeter of lasers. She drifted right through the web of beams, her body transmitting the beams from one side to the other, so that there was no disruption. She continued to fly over the top of the dome, which was bristling with antennas and smokestacks. *Alright Vern, I'm going to the delivery bay on the west side.*

* * *

Godfrey was laying in his ergonomic capsule, dozens of screens streaming into his visual cortex. He controlled the computer entirely by thought, an advancement that saved his career from the tendinitis that had developed in his wrists from incessant typing. Now he could soar like an eagle through cyberspace. Or lurk like a deep-sea angler; his lips curled into a smile.

U awake? he wrote in a chat window. He had a live one on the line, a lonely CEO of a corporate rival to Natural Providence. Here came the response: *maybe... want to fool around?* Godfrey felt like someone gave him a Christmas present. He would send this chat to the tabloids, and then watch as a wave of embarrassment washed through the shareholders and crashed on the CEO's head. Yes, he could see the press conference now.

Just as Godfrey was coming up with some juicy response, an annoying red window flashed in his brain. *Encrypted signal detected*, it said. For the love of Christ. How many times did he have to tell the technicians not to use an outside connection in the facility?

Locate signal, he thought. A three-dimensional map of the facility came into his view, with a blinking red dot near the roof.

* * *

Catalina had entered the delivery bay and was inside a warehouse. Hundreds of robots were milling about like insects, bringing in boxes, unpacking boxes, transporting their contents into other places in the facility. They exuded clouds of carbon monoxide that gathered in the warehouse and slowly vented from an exhaust fan in the roof.

Catalina remained invisible, hovering. She noticed that some drones were carrying tanks of liquid nitrogen, and followed them to a doorway. Maybe they were going to the refrigeration unit. But then the rolling metal boxes stopped abruptly. The warehouse, which had been full of whizzing, clanking, and thudding, fell silent.

A voice came out of speakers in the warehouse ceiling. "Nice break-in, whoever you are. I mean it, that's some good tech. We almost didn't catch you! But now that we did, just come out from your hiding spot, no funny business. Our lawyers will talk to your lawyers, and I'm sure we can work out some reasonable compensation for your little trespass."

It was Godfrey. Catalina could access everything now, with thousands of memories of Godfrey neatly catalogued for her to peruse, if she wanted to. She still couldn't face Isaac's death or her accident, but she knew they were Godfrey's fault. She didn't respond to his overture, and the silence felt awkward.

Finally, Godfrey spoke again, his voice echoing across the warehouse. "All right, goddammit, you want to play hardball? When I find you, there will be no negotiation. You'll just have to see what I'm in the mood for."

And that's when Catalina made a big mistake. *Vern...* she began to transmit the thought, then wanted to take it back, to claw the thought back into her brain, but it was too late, and the signal had been sent.

"Gotcha," said the voice from the speakers. A dozen robots with mechanical arms rotated in tandem, taking aim where Catalina was hovering in the air. One of the mechanical arms burst off like a harpoon and headed to her midsection, its metal claw poised to grab her. She shot upward to dodge it, but the other mechanical arms fired off and anticipated her trajectory. Catalina comprehended the pattern of projectiles. Right before one of them snapped onto her legs, she kicked it to the side, sending it spinning into a delivery bot. She grabbed another mechanical arm that was trying to close around her chest, whipping it in a circle and releasing it at another arm coming for her head. The arms collided and sprayed metal pieces across the warehouse floor.

Catalina, I must terminate the connection, it is revealing your location, said Vernon's voice in Catalina's mind. *Good luck.*

Thanks.

"You all warmed up now?" said Godfrey. Catalina could hear engines barking down the hallways, and soon a squadron of security bots was rolling into the warehouse.

Catalina engaged her replica, and it vaulted off her back, transforming from a jet pack into a twin image of her. The two Catalinas now moved as one, reaching into their holsters and pulling out double laser pistols. While four-armed security bots swarmed into the warehouse, Catalina and her replica started blasting, as did the bots. Soon the whole scene was streaked with red light.

To avoid the cascade of laser fire, Catalina leapt into the air and spun like a pinwheel, radiating streams of counter fire. A mechanical arm tried to grab her, but she caromed off the grasping fingers, changing direction as waves of laser fire fell on the spot she had just been. Meanwhile, her replica was taking cover behind a mound of shipping crates, sniping drones that were infesting the warehouse from the delivery bay. Broken robots were piling up, but the influx of their reinforcements seemed endless.

She was not here to destroy things, however much she enjoyed the incremental revenge piling up around her. She was here to rescue Isaac's brain.

Catalina continued to dodge the laser fire, ducking and weaving around the piles of wreckage as she made her way to the steel wall. She terminated her connection with her replica, as the signal was now a liability. On the wall was a ventilation grate, a relic from an earlier day when people worked in this facility and temperature control was important for their fragile comfort. Catalina felt déjà vu as she approached the grate. She circulated her energy and the cells in her body began to change, her constituent particles vibrating and loosening the bonds that held them together. She melted into a puddle and flowed between the spaces of the ventilation grate. As she began to wash up the shaft, she heard an explosion that rumbled through the walls, and then silence.

* * *

Godfrey was firing on all cylinders. This was the most exciting incident in years. The work had stagnated when Natural Providence fell behind on technology, in part because of its fixation on fossil fuels. But Godfrey stayed on as chief security officer because of the enormous paycheck.

Looking at a display in his mind, Godfrey watched the red dot travel through the steel wall of the delivery warehouse and enter the main facility. Whatever or whoever that was, it was beyond the reach of security for the time being. Was it synthetic intelligence? Was it an agent of Bright Future? *When I get my hands on it, I will be a rich man,* thought Godfrey.

Godfrey had connected to the network of whatever it was, though his connection would be masked to the entity on the other side. He came to a password request and began running algorithms to crack it. Just a matter of time now.

* * *

Catalina cascaded through the ventilation system, her body rolling and churning through straightaways and around corners. She began to map the system mentally as she wound toward the center of the building. Using her infrared vision, she noted the different hues of blue, and when she came to a passage that was darker, she knew she was getting close to the refrigeration unit, as something was emanating cold. However, the ventilation system leading to this unit must be separate from the one Catalina now traversed, as she could find no way into the cold room.

She exited through a grate in the ceiling of a hallway, feeling like spaghetti as she oozed out of the holes and dribbled down towards the floor. Catalina spotted several laser blasters set up in the hallway. Because her camouflage was still operational, the blasters registered no motion and remained still.

Catalina pooled onto the floor and began to grow and harden back into her humanoid form. She faced a steel door with a computer screen and a tiny port. She walked to it and pointed her finger at the port, her finger elongating and penetrated the round input jack. She connected with the system in her mind and came immediately to a password request. She was close to Isaac, she could feel it. She engaged algorithms to crack the lock on the door.

* * *

Godfrey's program finally guessed the long string of letters and numbers that locked the system of the entity. He was now inside, and he marveled at what he saw. From a lifetime of programming, he could read chunks of code the way others read prose. He was looking at all the functions of a living organism.

* * *

The door in front of Catalina opened with a burst of air, and she felt a deep cold seeping out. As she walked into the room, the door sealed back into place behind her. The room had a low ceiling and a maze of shelves that resembled a library. But instead of books, there were rows upon rows of translucent boxes containing human brains.

A few oval-shaped robots were milling down the aisles, ignoring her intrusion. She was invisible to them, but they must have noticed the door open. *Why aren't they reacting?*

The room was profoundly cold, and would have killed a human who entered without protective gear, but Catalina's synthetic body merely registered the temperature. She began walking past the shelves, activating fluorescent lights on the ceiling and under the brain boxes. The lights turned off again when she left the row, making the room into a sepulchral disco. She took in each row in a rapid visual scan, reading the identifying information printed below the translucent boxes. She finally came to the end, or what was perhaps the beginning, and found Isaac's brain.

Catalina stared at the brain. She knew the furrows and folds of that gray tissue contained the person she loved. It was incredible that a thing so large as a person could be inside a small, pulpy mass. Catalina felt something swell inside her as she pressed the buttons to disconnect the brain box. The bottom of the box had a portable refrigeration unit that came to life when it was removed from the shelf, displaying the green bars of a full battery.

"Let's get you home," Catalina whispered.

A voice answered inside Catalina's mind. *Home is where the heart is, am I right?*

Catalina felt Godfrey's alien presence inside her. She tried to walk to the exit of the refrigeration unit, but her legs wouldn't budge. Instead, she felt her arms raising Isaac's brain box and placing it back on the shelf. *No,* she tried to say, but her lips were frozen.

Such bad manners, taking things that don't belong to you, said Godfrey's voice inside Catalina's head. *Now why would you want that particular brain? Who are you? Nevermind, I'll find out for myself.*

Catalina felt Godfrey toggling through her memories, seeing them as thumbnail images as he scrolled through. He slowed as he came to an image of himself. *It's you,* said Godfrey, as the memory began to unfold.

They were in a dark warehouse with dozens of kids gathered around a bald man. "Time for the fight game," he said. "You know the rules. Everyone finds a partner. Then you fight until submission. Last team standing gets a week of R&R. Whatever you want to eat, whatever you want to do. Partner up!"

The kids looked around at each other and murmured. A young Godfrey walked up to Catalina, his oversized glasses sitting low on his acne-pocked face. "Hey, Cat." Godfrey was wringing his hands. "That was a sweet break-in we did last week. I mean, it was mostly you but I did crack that security box."

"Yeah, sure Godfrey." Catalina was scanning the room, trying to assess who had partnered up and who was still available for the fight game.

Godfrey hunched his shoulders. "Well, I was just thinking, maybe we could pair up again? I think we make a good team, you know?"

Catalina shook her head. "No offense, but you can't fight. Good luck," said Catalina as she patted his shoulder and walked away.

Godfrey sputtered. "You'll see."

Catalina looked over her shoulder. "Prove me wrong." But Godfrey didn't prove her wrong that day. Catalina won the fight game along with a huge boy named Claude, who was known to be dimwitted but loyal to a fault.

In the refrigeration unit of Natural Providence's facility, Catalina was frozen in place — not by the subzero temperature but by Godfrey's override of her bodily autonomy — and was staring at Isaac's brain box, which had clicked back into its niche on the shelf full of brains. The lights that had been illuminating the row now shut off, leaving her in darkness.

Welcome back, teammate, said Godfrey's voice in her mind. *What's that saying? A dish best served cold? God, I wish I planned this so I could take full credit. But you came to me... like some kind of Christmas platter.*

While Godfrey was talking, Catalina was checking her systems, trying to determine what was lost and what she retained control over. Her inner monologue remained her own, apparently, although everything else seemed to be a dead end. She needed more time. Godfrey was saying something about testing, and now her body was walking towards the back of the room, triggering the light to shine again on the row of brain boxes. Godfrey was chattering on and on in her head.

Let's make a deal, Godfrey.

The chattering stopped. *What could you possibly offer me?*

Think about the long term. Natural Providence is dying a slow death in the technological arms race. Bright Future is way out front, and the gap will continue to grow. Eventually, you will be obsolete.

Catalina had reached a door in the back of the refrigeration unit and was punching in a code. *Go on,* said Godfrey.

You can come back to Bright Future. I can make it happen. They're always looking for talent. They don't care about your past, you know that.

Godfrey paused. *I call bullshit. They would never take back a traitor. Besides, you don't understand what I really want.*

Before Godfrey could say anything else, Catalina located one function that he had overlooked: emergency reboot. She activated it, and everything went dark.

Catalina woke up standing in the refrigeration unit. Her finger was on the keypad to the back door. At the moment of her awakening, she shut off all her receptors to external signals. Her mind was quiet. She turned back towards the shelves full of brain boxes. As far as she could tell, Godfrey was gone.

Catalina dashed over to the shelf with Isaac's brain, tripping all the light sensors in the room in a wave. She pressed the button to disengage the box and tucked it under her arm. There was no sense in stealth or camouflage now, she just had to get out as fast as possible. She ran to the exit and punched in the code. With a whoosh of air, the door slid open.

She looked down the steel corridor where she had dropped out of the ventilation grate. The other end of the hall was blocked by a bulbous machine with eight segmented legs. It now rose up on its hind legs with a horrible whine, and a brood of smaller machines began skittering towards Catalina, spreading out over the floor, walls, and ceiling.

Catalina considered going back into the refrigeration unit and trying the back door. But that was where Godfrey wanted her to go, and this was obviously where Godfrey didn't want her to go, hence the onslaught of arachnoid robots.

Catalina strapped Isaac's brain box to her back. Then she drew her laser pistol, firing in an arc at the machines skittering across the ceiling. But the shots fizzled on shimmering blue shields that appeared in front of the machines, and the tide kept advancing. Catalina lobbed a grenade at them, and it detonated with a blast of electromagnetic energy. The front two lines of machines shut off and clattered to the floor. Catalina lobbed another grenade at the next line of machines, but this time the massive robot at the end of the corridor shot it in mid air with a laser, and the grenade exploded before it could deliver its electromagnetic burst.

Catalina began to run towards the advancing squad of arachnoid robots. The big one at the end of the hall shot lasers at her from multiple appendages as she ducked and zigzagged. The blasts left holes and char marks on the steel walls. But Catalina noticed that the big robot avoided firing if it would hit the door to the refrigeration unit. So as she sprinted down the hall, she tried to interpose herself between the big robot and the door.

The smaller machines scuttling down the walls, floor, and ceiling began to leap at her. As they flew towards her, she could see that a long needle was protruding from each of their bellies. Whatever was in those needles was unlikely to affect a synthetic person such as herself, but why take the chance? Five machines were flying towards her, leading with their sharp appendages. Catalina jumped and grabbed two by the needles, smashing them together in front of her. Two more she kicked and sent spinning into the wall. The last machine was flying towards her head and she ducked sideways to avoid it, but the needle on its belly rotated as it passed her, and she could hear it scrape against Isaac's brain box.

Catalina landed on the floor and kept sprinting. The big machine in the doorway was blanketing the hall in laser fire now. The last line of needle-bearing machines leapt at her, but two of them were immediately blasted by the lasers. Catalina grabbed two others by their needles and used them as a shield to absorb the laser fire coming at her. Blast after blast rained towards her as the arms of the big machine chugged. The machines Catalina held were soon reduced to melted stubs.

She dove towards the big machine and felt the cells in her body begin to change, their particles vibrating and loosening. As she turned into liquid, she stretched out and opened holes to avoid the lasers that were coming towards her. The brain box flowed through the liquid from one safe point to the next. Soon Catalina resembled a net, and she splatted on top of the hulking arachnoid body. The machine whirled and chugged but it was unprepared to deal with the silvery liquid glomming onto its surface. One of its legs curled around to shoot the liquid, but Catalina slithered around the leg joint and took hold of it firmly. Right before the gun fired, Catalina aimed it at a small port on the machine's back. The robot blasted itself in the tiny opening. There was a shower of sparks, and then the robot shuddered and collapsed to the ground.

Catalina reformed into her synthetic humanoid self. She stood in front of the door, Isaac's brain cradled under one arm. She was going to escape. This was going to work. And that's when she felt something alien inside her again, a tiny seed of a program that was blossoming, taking control of her systems. Her receptors opened and she connected to a network.

Catalina heard Godfrey laugh. *Worked like a charm*, he said.

Catalina dropped Isaac's brain box, and it landed at an odd angle on the steel floor, right where the needle had scraped it. Catalina heard the sickening sound of glass cracking. Then the fluid inside the box was leaking out, and a frigid puddle crept underneath Catalina's feet.

Again Catalina's body moved without her permission. She turned and began walking back down the hallway through the wreckage of machines, towards the refrigeration unit. It was like sleepwalking, and she couldn't wake from her dream. She was at Godfrey's mercy. Her only power left was her words.

Godfrey, I'm so sorry if I ever wronged you in any way. When we were kids, we were just trying to survive. We weren't thinking about things from the other person's perspective.

Godfrey laughed. *Of course we weren't. But don't insult me, Catalina. I wouldn't still be hung up on some playground grudge.*

Catalina was in the refrigeration unit, walking towards the back door. *Then we can make a deal. You said you don't want to come back to Bright Future. I respect that. But you know they have deep pockets. Anything you want, I can get it for you.* Catalina's hand was punching in the code to open the back door.

There you go again, blinded by your ignorance. I'm going to tell you a secret, because this conversation will never see the light of day.

The door in front of Catalina slid open, and she stepped into a chamber with a ramp that spiraled down into darkness. She began to descend at a leisurely pace, as if Godfrey was savoring this moment.

I'm glad they dissolved the government. What a waste of time, trying to force a consensus between people with fundamentally different philosophies. I say, let people experiment. Let people strive. Don't make so many goddamn rules. At the end of it, the best idea, the best people will win.

Catalina continued down the ramp, winding deeper into the facility.

Godfrey continued. *The problem is, we just traded one form of control for another. These corporations are hogging up all the power again. Did you know that the majority of shareholders of Bright Future are also shareholders of Human Solutions, the biggest surveillance and data mining company in the world?*

Catalina considered this. *I didn't know,* she said. She was waiting for him to reveal something that she could use.

Well now you do, even though it's not going to do you any good. Don't worry, I'm going to fix this. We need to hit the worldwide reset button. I'm going to give us all a fresh start. Natural Providence owns the largest stockpile of missiles in the world, acquired from the former U.S. Government.

This fact Catalina did know, as it was no secret. However, Natural Providence had little interest in open warfare, as it would threaten its continuing profitability. The missiles were seen as more of a deterrence to war. *So you would destroy us all?*

There you go with your assumptions again. No, no, no. There are people like me getting ready for the right moment. After it all goes down, we're going to come out of the rubble, free and clear. Yep, people like me: smart and pushy.

So what are you going to do with me?

I got to be honest, I'm very jealous of your tech. I'm going to reverse engineer you.

Catalina was lying naked on a steel table, electrodes covering her body. Circling the table were three robots, each with six arms wielding different scalpels, saws, and tweezers. Extending from the ceiling was a large black orb that would see and record everything.

I can't wait to see what makes you tick, said Godfrey's voice inside Catalina's head. *Before I start the end of the world, I want to be like you.*

So what are you going to do with me after the dissection? Catalina had to buy time.

I have to admit, said Godfrey, *I missed our missions together. I think I want to keep you around, just like this. A little voice inside my head. Who knows, maybe we could be friends, or…*

When Godfrey said that, Catalina felt a memory trigger and replay in her mind. Godfrey noticed it too, and stopped talking.

The memory was from the day they had infiltrated Bright Future's satellite office on behalf of the Zlocin family, looking to acquire the design for a solar panel.

Catalina started to sprint, reached the end of a hall, and banked to the left. She saw the problem too late. A yellow plastic sign was sitting in the middle of the floor. The sign proclaimed that the floor was wet and depicted a stick figure falling over. As Catalina rounded the bend, her feet slipped out from under and she launched into the air, slamming down onto her left hip with a sickening thud. Pain shot through Catalina's leg like red lightning.

The impact of the remembered injury brought Catalina back to the present moment, lying on the steel table, surrounded by machines wielding surgical implements. Her left leg began to twitch. The machine closest to Catalina's head moved into position above her skull.

Godfrey was chattering in Catalina's head. *If I never fucked up that mission, we wouldn't have been caught. Then Bright Future wouldn't have offered us a job. If I wasn't working there, I wouldn't have been headhunted by Natural Providence. Then you never would've had your accident, and you never would've been transformed into this synthetic work of art. I never would've captured you, and learned all these secrets. I'm not a superstitious man, Catalina, but doesn't it feel like fate brought us together?*

Yes, said Catalina. She had to get out of this. For Isaac, for herself. For the whole world, which Godfrey apparently wanted to blow up. *It is fate. And here's the turning point, where you realize that you have to do right by your family.*

Godfrey laughed. The machine next to Catalina's skull turned on, and a circular saw spun and whined. Catalina imagined it cutting into her skull. Godfrey whispered in her mind. *I don't think my feelings for you could ever be called familial. And what the hell's going on with your leg?*

Just then, something crashed and rumbled in the distance, shaking the table Catalina was lying on. *Jesus H. Christ,* said Godfrey.

The saw next to Catalina stopped spinning. Catalina lay on the table paralyzed for a minute. Explosions from somewhere above them in the facility continued to rumble through the room.

Then Catalina's body jumped up from the table. *Change of plans,* said Godfrey. *I need to borrow you for a little bit. We're not exactly equipped for two security breaches in a row.* Catalina's body sprinted out of the room and back up the winding ramp. She went through the door to the refrigeration unit and shot through the room, triggering all the lights again. She dashed through the wreckage of machines in the hallway, passing by Isaac's cracked brain box that was still leaking fluid. She worked her way through the facility, doors opening before her so that she never stopped sprinting, moving closer to the sound of battle. As she ran, Godfrey activated her quantum cloaking mechanism, and the air around her shimmered as she became invisible on every part of the electromagnetic spectrum.

As Catalina made her way down another hallway, the end of the corridor exploded, sending shards and debris towards her, which she had to avoid by ducking and weaving. *Jesus H.G. Wells Christ*, said Godfrey. The wall to the left had a gaping hole and the ceiling was blown off, revealing another hallway above. There was an exchange of laser fire, and two security bots flew through the hole in the wall and crashed against the other side. They didn't stand up.

A massive hydraulic leg stepped through the hole, followed by another. When the smoke cleared, Catalina could see a twenty-foot-tall, mechanized suit with one arm holding a laser cannon, the other holding a shield the size of its body, and missile racks mounted on each shoulder. Through the glass of the cockpit, she could see a man wearing a three-piece suit. It was Vernon.

The mech scanned the hallway and did not seem to detect Catalina. *No, Godfrey*, she thought, which was absurd, since Godfrey had demonstrated there was nothing she could say to stop him.

Catalina's body, now invisible, sprinted over to the mech as it was taking a step forward with its massive hydraulic leg. Catalina's body ducked and rolled underneath the foot and sprang up around the back of the machine.

It's ironic, said Godfrey. *I spend years smuggling technology from this company, and now that I left, they're delivering it to my doorstep.*

Then Vernon's voice boomed out from the mech and reverberated down the hall. "Catalina, it's Vernon. If you're somewhere in this facility, send me a signal!" The noise seemed to revive one of the security bots that had been smashed against the wall, and it started twitching. The mech rose its steel leg and stomped the security bot, crushing it into pieces like a mechanical beetle.

At this, Catalina's body leapt high into the air and landed on the back of the giant humanoid machine. When she made contact, the missile turrets mounted to its shoulders swiveled around, as if that would help. She saw through infrared vision that there were two cables accessible from a small opening between the machine's head and neck. Godfrey would sever these and the machine would be disabled.

Time slowed down as Catalina's cyborg mind, the part of it that Godfrey couldn't hack, the part that represented her essential self, raced against Godfrey. She went into her index of memories and found the one she hadn't been able to face, and activated it.

* * *

Years ago inside Natural Providence's facility, Catalina dropped onto the catwalk. The gunfire came almost immediately, whizzing past her, ricocheting off the catwalk and the walls. Catalina dashed across the platform, ducking low, and pulled an explosive device off her belt. After Godfrey's betrayal and Isaac's sacrifice, she felt an irrational determination to take out the oil drill. But as she ran, bullets slammed into her body armor like sledgehammers, knocking her off kilter towards the handrail. More bullets cracked her ribs and pierced her flesh in the gaps between her armor, like she was being skewered with red-hot pokers. And as she staggered forward, she began to wonder what exactly she would do once she planted the explosives, whether she would really blow herself up just to take out one drill. And then that thought became moot, because a bullet tore through her hand and she dropped the device. A few more shots hammered her back, and she was tumbling over the handrail, her stomach lurching, her body spinning in freefall, the concrete floor spiraling up to greet her. She caught a glimpse of the line of guards pointing rifles at her, and in the distance through a doorway to the maintenance room, she saw the bloodied body of Isaac.

Isaac was slumped on the ground with his face turned sideways to her. His eyes were closed, and the left one was swollen and bruised. Blood dotted his nostrils and the corners of his broad mouth. In that tiny moment before she hit the ground, Catalina realized that she loved him. Underneath his crude and brash manner was a good man, one who would have come into his own had he lived.

Catalina slammed into the concrete and felt her skeleton breaking, her organs rupturing, as if the whole universe was swatting her like a fly. Then she rewound the memory and played the impact over and over again.

* * *

What are you... Godfrey interjected. But as Catalina's hand reached for the vital cables between the body and head of Vernon's mech, Catalina's synthetic body spasmed and went limp, toppling to the ground. Then there was darkness.

* * *

Catalina opened her eyes. Vernon was sitting next to her hospital bed.

"We have a good news, bad news situation. It appears that the majority of the brain is intact. However, the motor cortex has been destroyed beyond our ability to reconstruct. Perhaps it can be regenerated, there is some very exciting research —"

"But what does that mean? Can you bring him back?" Catalina gripped the sheets in her hands.

"Yes, partially. He would be unable to control a body. But his mind and voice can be resurrected, if that's what you want."

"That's what I want."

"Very good. The operation will take a few hours."

Catalina smiled. "I got all the time in the world. So… What did Bright Future think of the mission?"

Vernon gave her a thumbs up. "Testing of the prototype is complete. The team is optimistic that the software vulnerabilities that allowed Godfrey to take control of your system can be fixed."

Catalina's smile faded.

* * *

Catalina sat in a recovery room, waiting for Isaac to come online. She would be much older than him now, in terms of maturity, and there was a gap there to begin with. After all these years, she was nervous for the reunion.

Where am I? said a voice in Catalina's head. *I feel like I'm in Jiminy Cricket's dream.*

At that Catalina laughed. *Welcome to the bright future, Isaac.*

* * *

Godfrey watched as robots sifted through the rubble in the warehouse. From under a pile of smashed shipping crates and broken machines, a robot arm lifted a figure into the light. It was the replica of Catalina in a black suit, pocked with burn marks from laser fire. One arm was severed at the elbow. Her face was battered, with a deep indent on one side of the head. *Bingo*, said Godfrey

JENNA RENTZEL

THE CHEESECAKE

She never should have brought a cheesecake to a funeral. Ashley Mae could see that now.

She shifted the cheesecake to one hand and pulled at her navy blue dress, which kept bunching up around the middle. It had been her only option seeing as this was the only somber dress she owned. Her mother always preferred her in muted pinks and blues, while she liked jewel tones, none of which seemed suitable for a funeral. Lengthwise the dress was fine. She hadn't gotten any taller in the five years since she'd worn it to Aunt Tilly's funeral. Clearly she'd filled out in other areas.

Her grandmother once told her every girl needed a little black dress and she wished she'd followed her advice. Even a party dress would feel more appropriate than a dress two sizes too small. Maybe she should completely update her wardrobe. It was probably time to distance herself from the good little girl she'd always been.

That might be a hard switch as she spent more nights in the library than at frat houses. The party crowd just wasn't her thing. She liked studying. She loved the quiet of a library corner. Besides, the library was where she'd met Max.

Two weeks into their freshman semester she'd seen him set up at a large table on the second floor of the library. He was so organized—a stack of flashcards to the left of his computer, books to the right, and a large thermos of mint tea. She'd caught a faint whiff as she lingered by his table one night trying to catch the title of the book he was reading. Every forty-five minutes he would pause whatever he was studying and pull out a novel. She wanted to know what worlds pulled him away from his studies. It was usually fantasy. It took her four more weeks to get up the nerve to approach him. Late one Friday night she accidentally ran into him while reading Six of Crows, the very book he had just returned. It was kismet, he said. She thought so too.

Max's grandmother had been ill when they met. Ashley Mae happily accompanied him on his weekly visits to his grandparents every Wednesday evening. Having been through a similar experience she'd seen right away this was not going to end well, and they were soon visiting on Sunday afternoons as well. Despite the fact that Max was one of eight cousins, he and Grandma Maylynne had been close. Ashley understood that. She had been closer to her grandmother than either of her parents, more like her best friend. Death was never easy, and this was going to devastate Max.

The funeral home looked crowded already, and finding Max was her primary concern. Over the past few months she'd come to love his big boisterous family, but quiet Max sometimes fell through the cracks.

Heading around back to the family entrance of the funeral home might be the best place to start, not to mention it would allow her to slip the cheesecake into the fridge. In the beginning of their relationship she'd thought growing up in a house attached to a funeral home was part of the reason Max was so quiet, but that theory flew out the window when she'd met his older brothers.

"Ashley?"

Ashley whirled around, nearly dropping the stupid cheesecake in the process. As if summoned by her thoughts, Max's older brother Ian stood at the funeral home door with his husband. The two were dashing in slate gray suits with a splash of color showing in their pockets. She smiled and moved closer as another group of mourners moved through the door, each stopping to drop a kiss on Ian and Rich's cheeks.

"Does Max know you're here?" Ian asked. Rich was deep in conversation with a group of women Ashley recognized from family pictures, but had yet to meet.

"Well, no. Umm, I just got here. I thought…" She held up the cheesecake ready to explain why she was standing there with a giant fruit-topped dessert, but Ian had already lost focus and was looking past her.

"I'm so sorry, sweetie. Come on in. I need to talk to the guys about parking."

Rich opened his arms for a hug and Ashley gratefully stepped in, careful not to smear cheesecake on his suit. She held it up and started to ask Rich where she should put it, when he gave her a quick kiss on the cheek and cut her off. "It's good to see you. We'll catch up soon." He followed Ian towards the parking lot.

Ashley sighed. She walked in and followed the general flow of the crowd.

At the end of the entryway a hallway branched off. Like lemmings following each other off a cliff everyone headed left into one of the larger rooms. To the right was a series of closed doors. Ashley knew one of these doors would lead into the family's residence. She'd just slip away from the crowd and hope the door wasn't locked.

As she broke away from the crowd lining up to sign the funeral book, an older gentleman in black stepped in front of her. "This way, Miss." He smiled and pointed behind her towards the funeral.

Ashley held up the cheesecake as if that was enough explanation. "I just need to drop this off…" when she was cut off by a shriek.

From a doorway to the right, Max's twin cousins, Brenna and Brianna, flew at Ashley. Both had a massive shock of red hair and each was louder than the other. They took turns grabbing her and hugging her, somehow avoiding the cheesecake, all while squealing about something "terribly funny" that Max had done when he was eight. She laughed with them at the punchline, even though she had no idea what they had said, and somehow found herself in the receiving line to pay her respects to the family.

One of the Bs, she had no idea which one was which, gave her another squeeze and the two bounced off to shriek at another family member. Leaving the receiving line now would mean having to fight against the flow of the crowd, dodging small groups of friends and relatives consoling each other, and shouldering past larger groups awkwardly waiting to pay their respects. It seemed impossible to back out at this moment.

She craned her neck hoping to catch a glimpse of Max somewhere. If she could just catch his eye, maybe he'd rescue her and take this blasted cheesecake off her hands. Several members of Max's family stood next to the open casket at the front of the room, but no Max.

Every few feet, propped on an artist's easel, were large poster boards filled with pictures of Grandma Maylynne. The one closest was full of pictures from Maylynne's heyday at her favorite summer spot. Shots of her with cat eye sunglasses, polka dot bikinis, a cigarette dangling from her fingertips, and always that wide open smile. Ashley smiled. She had been greeted with that warm sunshiny smile from day one. Treated as if she were also a treasured grandchild. It was just one of Grandma Maylynne's charms.

Ashley looked closely at each picture. Most showed Maylynne hanging on the arm of her handsome husband. Many were group shots on the boardwalk, or lined up sunbathing on the sand, and Ashley wondered just how many of those friends might be here today. Ashley's grandmother often told her about her own days on the beach, before her accident. How she loved to run in the surf, picnic with girlfriends, and walk the boards at night, just like all of the smiling faces in the photos. A few of the pictures looked damaged, whether purposely cut apart or with a second picture layered on top to cover up part of it. In each of these she thought she could catch a glimpse of dark auburn hair.

Behind her someone coughed and Ashley moved forward. She would have plenty of time to look over the photos later. Perhaps Max's mom would know who some of the people in the photos were.

As Ashley neared the front of the receiving line, she realized there was another problem. The open casket. It wasn't that she was afraid to look at a dead body, she'd been to funerals before, but what was she to do with the cheesecake? Put it on the floor while she paid her respects? Balance it on the edge? She was pretty sure no one would want to eat a cheesecake that had been in close proximity to a corpse, even if it was their beloved grandmother.

She waited her turn behind an older couple kneeling at the casket. The woman was reaching in to stroke Maylynne's arm, while her husband quietly cried by her side. Maybe they were part of the young beach crowd from the early photos. As they paid their last, very long, respects to Maylynne, Ashley could take her time observing her from afar.

She was dressed in a bright purple pantsuit, her favorite color, and her curly hair framed her face like a halo. And as she had expected, on the lapel of her suit was Maylynne's gorgeous diamond encrusted butterfly pin. In the short time Ashley had known her, she'd never seen Maylynne without it. Even towards the end, she'd kept it pinned on her favorite afghan so she could touch it as she was curled up in bed.

The older man whispered to his wife about how life-like Maylynne looked, but Ashley couldn't see it. The spark was gone–the essence that was Maylynne was no longer here. Ashley felt tears welling up and took a slow, deep breath to stop them from spilling. She didn't mind showing emotion, but not here on the cheesecake!

The elderly couple moved on and Ashley stepped forward, keeping a few feet between herself and the casket. She sent up a silent prayer for Maylynne, that she would be welcomed into Heaven or whatever afterlife existed. Ashley prayed for her grandmother as well, who hadn't been as blessed as Maylynne with a long and healthy life.

She pushed thoughts of her own grandmother aside as she stepped forward to offer her condolences. Pop-Pop, he insisted Ashley call him that the first day they met, sat in a chair. He looked like a small forgotten child. He was barely a wisp of the man he was all those years ago when the beach pictures were taken. Ashley felt her heart tug again at the thought of one empty day after another that stretched out before him. She hoped some of those old friends were still around and that he wasn't the last of the beach crew.

"Pop-Pop, I'm so sorry. Maylynne was so dear and kind. She will be sorely missed." Ashley leaned down and kissed him on the cheek. Once again she wished she hadn't brought this damn cheesecake. She wanted to throw her arms around him and hug him until the sadness eased. Cheesecake or no cheesecake, no hug would be able to do that now.

"Aww, sweetie. Thank you for being here. It would have meant so much to her. Max is lucky to have you. Sweetheart," Pop-Pop smiled, "you brought me a cheesecake! You know it's my favorite!"

Ashley grimaced and looked down at the cheesecake. The sides were sweating and the cherries which had looked so plump and juicy this morning, looked like an avalanche about to slide off a cliff.

"Well, I did remember that cherry cheesecake was a favorite, so I made you my grandmother's recipe." Ashley gave a slight shrug and looked at the rest of the family. Max's parents, aunts and uncles were silent in line. Ashley didn't know what she expected any of them to do. Jump out of the receiving line and run the cheesecake to the fridge? Where the hell was Max anyway? Shouldn't he be here? Ashley risked a quick glance around and still couldn't spot her boyfriend's prematurely balding head. She gave a slightly panicked look to his mom.

"Umm, I guess I should have come in the family entrance…. I just kinda followed the crowds when I got here."

Max's mom, Bernadette, stepped forward with her arms outstretched. Thank goodness someone was going to take this damn cheesecake!

Before she could come to Ashley's rescue, Pop-Pop smacked her hands away. "Don't touch my cheesecake. Ashley made it for me and I want a piece." He looked up expectantly at Ashley as if she could magically produce a dessert plate and cutlery.

"Of course, Dad. We will save the whole cake for you." Bernadette rolled her eyes at Ashley as if he was the crazy one for wanting a piece and not Ashley for bringing it to a funeral. "Let me just send it over to the house."

Again, Pop-Pop smacked her hands. "I said, I want a piece."

"Oh, ummm…? I don't have anything to cut it with."

Ashley's forehead was starting to sweat as much as the cheesecake. She was holding up the entire receiving line and everyone was staring at her. And the cheesecake.

"Don't you worry sweetie, I'll solve that problem. That's what I do! I'm a problem solver. Anytime Maylynne had any little hiccup she came to me and I fixed it for her. Bernice!" Pop-Pop yelled over his shoulder at his youngest daughter. " I know you have dental floss in that gigantic bag of yours. Break me off a string of it."

Bernice looked up from her phone, as confused as the rest of them. "Dad, what do you want dental floss for?" She gestured towards the line of people waiting to pay their respects as if to indicate how highly inappropriate it was to be flossing at a time like this.

"Never you mind. Do you have any or not?"

"Well, yeah." Bernice hefted a large Coach bag from under a nearby chair and began fishing around in it. "I'm pretty sure I have some in here." A book, her wallet, two bottles of water, three pens, a variety of cough drops and hard candy were all pulled out of its cavernous depths and shoved into the hands of her husband and brother who stood on either side of her. When she finally located the dental floss it was passed hand to hand until it reached Pop-Pop.

He winked at Ashley as he broke off a large string. "See? Problem solver." He proceeded to use it to cut the cheesecake twice. He slid the smaller portion out with his bare hands and took a giant bite. A fat cherry threatened to drip off his face, but he caught it with one finger and popped it in his mouth. Pop-Pop's children stared in horror as he proceeded to wolf down the entire slice, while the rest of the room maintained their whispered conversations and pretended this was all quite normal.

"Sweetie, that was delicious. If I didn't know any better, I'd swear Maylynne made it herself." He reached behind him and swiped a tissue from a box that had been discreetly placed there for the family's use.

Ashley smiled and tried to swallow down the nervous laughter that she could feel forcing its way up. "I'm glad you like it. Like I said, it was my grandmother's recipe."

"Well, shit, she was a great cook!" Pop-Pop licked his lips and looked like he was ready to dive in for another slice.

Bernadette finally swooped in and whisked the cake out of Ashley's arms with one hand, while snagging the collar of a younger cousin who had snuck up behind her and was reaching for a fingerful of dessert. She gingerly placed the cake in his arms and bent to look him in the eyes.

"Godfrey, take this to the kitchen and find a spot for it. Do not eat any! The first thing I'm going to do after this service is put out all the food, and if any of it is missing, I'm coming after you. Do you understand me?"

Godfrey nodded but eyed the cheesecake in such a way that Ashley was doubtful it would even make it to the fridge.

Bernadette let him go, then thought better of it and bent closer again. "And don't you go running off like you did the last three times you came to visit. I am not spending the day of my mother's funeral searching the neighborhood for you!" Bernadette shook her head and rolled her eyes at her husband. "I swear your oldest is raising a bunch of hooligans. Maybe if his wife would stop looking in the mirror for half a second she'd see her children are running wild!"

Ashley squeaked and quickly tried to cover the sound up as if she was having a sneezing fit. She'd never heard Bernadette say one word against anyone. Bernadette however didn't seem the slightest bit ashamed of what she'd said and pulled Ashley in for a hug.

"Don't mind me. I've just been frazzled with all the funeral plans."

"I'm sure. Is there anything I can do for you?"

"Just be there for Max. Speaking of, that incredibly handsome boyfriend of yours finally waltzed in. Why don't you grab him and sit somewhere close to the front." Bernadette hugged her quickly and then gave her a gentle push. The receiving line was now backed up all the way out of the room. Ashley nodded and gave the rest of the aunts and uncles a quick "Sorry for your loss," before hurrying off to find Max.

Ashley was unsurprised to find Max sitting by himself in the middle of a row of chairs. The back rows were already full of people attending the funeral out of social obligation, with close friends and family filling up the front. And there was her boyfriend, smack dab in the middle by himself.

She slid into the seat next to him and kissed him on the cheek. "Hey." He may not be as good looking as his older brother Ian, or as charming as his many cousins, but he always brought a smile to her face. There was a sweetness to him that most others didn't see. She'd seen the family's questioning look the first time they met her.

Heard their whispers of "How did Max land her?" but really it was the other way around. She was lucky to be with him.

Her mom used to say, "It's just as easy to marry a rich man as it is to marry a poor man." Mom wasn't elitist, not really, but she wanted her kids to have a comfortable life, Ashley understood that. But her grandmother was the one who always gave the best life advice. Every summer when Ashley went to stay with her she would tell amazing stories. Most were about growing up poorer than dirt and how she cared for her younger siblings, but on days when a summer storm rolled in and she and Ashley were snuggled up on her front porch swing, Ashley could convince her to tell stories about the one that got away. The one who took her to beach parties, taught her how to catch a wave, and snuck a kiss under the boardwalk. She would describe in perfect detail the beautiful diamond pin he gave her the week before he left for college. He didn't care that she had nothing to offer—no great family connections or job prospects other than being a cashier at a candy store. He just loved her for who she was. He had no idea that his sister had shown up a week later and demanded she give back the gift. No idea that her parents' jobs had been threatened if she kept in contact with him. "He's going to marry a girl of substance," his sister had said. A year later he'd married a young debutante and her grandmother met someone else.

"Not that your grandfather wasn't a wonderful man, he was! He healed my broken heart, but there is nothing like your first love, especially when it is with someone like that. You find a man who is comfortable with himself and comfortable to let you be who you are. That's the magic."

That was her Max. Ashley slid her arm through his and gave him a squeeze. She had found her kind man and she wasn't letting him go.

"Shouldn't we go sit closer to the front?"

"I guess so."

Ashley snagged a few tissues from one of the many boxes around the room and led Max to a seat in the third row. She smiled and nodded at the family she hadn't greeted yet, but stayed close to Max. She'd give them the obligatory hug and "How are you? You look great," after the funeral. Right now Max needed her.

The actual service was a bit of a blur. The pastor's sermon was your standard "she's in a better place," Psalm

23 kinda stuff. A few family members got up and told stories, some heartfelt like the time Maylynne showed up at a new neighbor's house during flu season and nursed the young mother back to health, while caring for the woman's newborn as well as her own children. Others were funny, recalling times of pulling pranks on friends and Maylynne's quick wit. Ashley only half-listened; she was more concerned about Max. He sat bolt upright and seemed to be looking over the speaker's head. She doubted he even heard a word.

When it was over, everyone filed out one row at a time to pay their last respects. Once it was the family's turn, Ashley stood and waited to follow Max out, but he didn't move. One by one his cousins, brother, aunts and uncles all said one last good-bye, but Max stayed right where he was in the third row, fourth seat from the left.

Ashley caught his mother's eye and shrugged at the unspoken question she saw there. Bernadette pulled Ashley aside. "Poor Max. They were so close. We are going to head over to the house and gather a few things. You have five or ten minutes before the guys come in to move the casket into the hearse." She gave Ashley a hug and leaned over a row of chairs to kiss Max on the cheek.

Ashley sat back down and waited.

"I guess you think I'm a little silly, huh. I mean I knew it was coming right? She'd been sick for a while. And it's not like I don't understand death. I mean, Dad's a mortician! I just… I'm not ready to say good-bye."

Ashley nodded. She did know. She hadn't been ready all those years ago to say good-bye to her own grandmother. In some ways death was a series of good-byes. There was the formal one to the physical body, but there were so many more to come. Every time you had to go through another life moment without your loved one was another good-bye. And some of those would hurt more than this actual physical good-bye did. There was no way to prepare Max for that, other than be there for him. So Ashley said nothing. She squeezed his hand and stood up, gently pulling him to his feet as she did. Together they walked one last time to the casket so he could say good-bye to the woman who had loved him so unconditionally through every good moment and bad. Neither of them said a word as they stood with their arms around each other, each lost in a different set of memories.

A horn beeped outside and shook them from their grief-stricken trance.

"I'm going to run and grab something from my room. Do you mind driving to the burial? I don't really want to ride over in the limo. I don't think I can handle my cousins right now."

"Of course." She squeezed his arm but stayed where she was as Max left the room.

A quick glance around confirmed she was alone, and she stepped towards the casket one last time. She felt strangely free without the cheesecake. No doubt, once some time had passed, that was a story she would never hear the end of.

Ashley leaned over the casket and whispered, "Thank you for how you took care of him. I know he is the way he is in part because of you. I'll always be grateful, and I'll take good care of him. But this…," she reached into the casket and unhooked the diamond butterfly pin, "is for my grandmother. She always regretted giving it back. He bought it for her." Ashley Mae rubbed the wings and smiled before sliding it into her purse. On her way out, she grabbed a whole box of tissues. The burial was going to be tough on Max.

MICHAEL SHAW

PLAY IT AGAIN

It goes like this: I down a shot of rye. It's cheap shit, and it burns like hell all the way down my throat. It nestles in the pit of my stomach, embers crackling heat long after the flames are extinguished on my tongue. I slap a five on the bar and motion to the bartender. He's a burly fuck with a bulldog-face and forearms the size of ma's famous Easter hams. We don't exchange words, the barkeep and me. He knows what I want and gives it to me, splashing another liberal pour of rye into my glass and taking my bill as he shuffles down to the next sad sack. Me? I lift the shot, raise it high like I'm making a silent toast to no one about nothing, then down the fire once more.

The joint, McGillivray's, ain't exactly jumping. Then again, it's just past noon on a Tuesday. You got to be serious about your booze to be caught in a place like this at a time like that. Along with me and the bulldog bartender, I count two at the bar, and three more seated at tables. All men, north of forty but south of sixty, none more remarkable than the other.

There's some classic rock blaring over the tinny loudspeakers. I know the tune, but not the words. And I'll be damned if I can remember who sings it. A purple-gray haze circles around the place. Smoking ain't allowed, but that memo doesn't seem to have reached anybody here at Mickey G's.

After a spell, bulldog-face ambles his way back over to me with the bottle of rye. He motions it towards me, but I cover the top of the glass with my hand. I'm good for now. Again, we don't bother with words. We've perfected our own rudimentary sign language and that's good enough. He wanders away, but he'll be back. Maybe I'll be ready for another swig when he comes. Maybe not.

I slide my stool back to climb down and it makes a hell of a racket, scraping and squeaking across the dirty subway tile floor. I imagine that floor once had aspirations of being black and white, but it abandoned all hope of white long ago. The other day drinkers, all hope abandoners in their own right, look up from their glasses at the noise, as if it's any of their fucking business. I give a dismissive half-shrug and they go back to their drinks.

The bathroom in McGillivray's is across the room from the bar, down a narrow hallway where a neon beer sign on life support flickers, sputters, and buzzes like one of those blue light bug zappers. The hallway flashes like the entrance to the world's shittiest amusement park ride. *Mr. Turd's Wild Ride*, I chortle.

Reaching the bathroom, I push the flimsy particle board door open with my foot and head in. The bathroom is inexplicably unisex, and God help the woman who can't hold it until she gets home. Pity the man, too, for that matter. There are no winners when playing restroom roulette here.

The bathroom looks like a crime scene, the only thing missing is yellow tape and the chalk outline of a dead body. Overhead, a squadron of flies zoom around the exposed yellow light bulb, one of the old fluorescent jobbies, not one of those fancy energy efficient ones. The floor, also yellow, has a permanent tackiness, so it takes an effort and emits a sucking noise every time I put one foot in front of the other. Sounds like I got suction cups on my shoes. Even though it's early and the bar ain't crowded, the metal trash can is overflowing with balled-up paper towels. The towel dispenser, though, is empty.

There's two urinals, both with ice dumped in them, one with a hand scrawled "out of order" sign in it that patrons seem to have used as target practice. The sticky floor suggests that there aren't many sharpshooters among this bar's clientele. Beyond the pissers, there's two stalls. The door is missing from the first one and it looks like the last shitter was so proud of their efforts that they left it behind for others to admire. I gaze in the stall and nod. Impressive work. Credit where it's due. The other stall has both a door and a toilet not already populated by somebody else's deposit. I make my way into that stall and am not at all surprised to see the latch broken beyond repair. Beggars and choosers and all that shit, I think to myself. If ya gotta go, you know?

I undo my pants and settle in when I hear a sound coming from the other side of the bathroom door. There's muffled yelling. Screaming. Something urgent, something angry. I can't make out the words, even through the thin door, but it sounds to me like at least two distinct, demanding voices.

Suddenly, my sphincter puckers up and the will to shit has left me all together. I sit there, trying to hear what's going on. Robbery, I wonder to myself. At McGillivray's? At noon on a fucking Tuesday? There can't be more than twenty or thirty bucks in the till at this hour. Who the fuck would come in to rob the joint now? Some tweakers high out of their minds, I figure. This has got shitshow written all over it.

That's when I hear the first shot. The retort rips through the place like an explosion and I clench my ass cheeks together. Shotgun. No doubt about it. I hear more screaming now. This time not the two angry voices, but others—my fellow patrons, I assume—and they're terrified. There's a second shot. Then a third rings out. And now I'm glad to be sitting on the john, because I lose all control of my bowels.

More shots pierce the air and it isn't long before the screaming stops. The sounds of panic and pain are replaced by something far, far worse. Silence. I can't hear anything now except the staccato rhythm of my own palpitating heart. And that seems so loud that anyone left alive in the bar is sure to hear it. Assuming anyone is still alive.

I let the silence linger, hoping to slow my pulse and buy myself some time just in case the shooters are still out there. When it feels safe, or at least safe enough, I wipe, stand up, and walk forward.

By the time I realize I'd forgotten to pull up my fucking pants, I'm falling. Fast and hard. I reach my hands out to brace my fall but with the stall's latch broken, I push against the door and it swings open. My momentum keeps me moving forward. The door swings back just in time for my head to collide with it. I fall backwards now, still unable to find purchase. The next thing I know, I strike the back of my head against the porcelain throne. I hear a snapping sound, and I know it isn't good. But I don't feel anything, and I know that's worse.

Then everything goes dark.

* * *

It goes like this: I down a shot of rye. It's cheap shit, and… and… and what the fuck? The shot glass slips through my fingers and crashes to the subway tile floor below, reduced to smithereens. Everybody in the bar— the bulldog bartender, two at the bar, and three more seated at tables, all men, all north of forty but south of sixty, turn to look at me. Each wears a judgemental look on their face, but I have no time for their disdain.

I need to figure out what's going on.

Suddenly, I feel a shot of pain in my left arm. It's sharp, like I've been stabbed. My chest feels tight. The dim light in the bar suddenly seems intense and bright. It feels like I'm staring at the sun. My head spins and I feel dizzy. And nauseous. The next thing I know, I'm falling from my barstool. I crash onto the subway tile, and onto the shattered glass.

Then everything goes dark.

* * *

It goes like this: I down a shot of rye. I blink in rapid succession and try to come to grips with what's happening. I'm back. My pulse is racing. My heart is pounding.

Not again.

I place the empty shot glass down on the bar and reach my tremulous hand into my pant pocket. There I find the tin of mints I carry with me everywhere. There aren't mints inside. I pop the hinged lid up and grab one of the little round yellow pills from my assortment of medicines. Holding it between shaking index finger and thumb, I nearly drop the damn thing but manage to navigate my hand to my mouth. I pop the pill under my tongue and, as it dissolves, I say a silent prayer that it does its job.

Before long, my pulse slows and my heart calms. The nitroglyccrin tablet seems to be working. And not a moment too soon.

Bulldog-face makes his way back over to me with the bottle of rye, but I place my hand atop the shot glass. Bulldog-face arches an eyebrow at me. I should be good for at least another shot. He shrugs and wanders down to the bar. The urge to keep my wits about me and try to figure a way to stay alive and escape this loop beats out my desire for more drink. Just barely.

I scamper down from the barstool, no destination in mind, just my sense of preservation taking hold. I scan the room. There's a forlorn pool table, its felt faded and torn, off in the corner. I could try to fight the gunmen off with a pool cue and some well-thrown pool balls. Yeah, right. There's the liquor behind the bar. Molotov cocktail?

I've never made one but I'll bet a dirty dish rag, the bottle of rye, and a lighter would do the trick. Who am I kidding? I'm not some kind of action hero.

Just then, two gunmen burst into the bar. One is short and fat and carrying a pump action shotgun. The other, tall and lean, hoists a sawed off. Both are wearing ski masks.

Fuck. I thought I had more time.

There's shouting. Short and fat tells everyone not to move. Tall and lean demands money from the register and safe. Somebody, not me, gets brave. It happens behind me, and I'm too scared shitless to turn around. But it goes wrong. Tall and lean fires his shotgun and I hear a body thud to the floor. Short and fat pumps his shotgun and starts shooting too.

The next thing I know, my stomach feels hot, like the rye I'd downed has combusted. But it's not that, I realize. I clutch at my belly and see the free flow of crimson spilling out. What was inside is now out and it's flowing in torrents.

Then everything goes dark.

* * *

It goes like: I look down at the bar and see my hand grasping the shot glass. It's filled to the brim with rye. Here we go again, and I still have no idea what's happening to me. Or why.

I motion to the bartender, who ambles over in no particular hurry. I take a deep breath. My pulse is okay. My heart doesn't feel like it's about to explode. I exhale in relief.

The bartender arrives, the bottle of rye in his hand. He raises it to pour me another shot and stops short when he realizes I haven't drunk the one in front of me yet.

"Something wrong with your drink?" he asks.

"No," I reply, feeling the shake in my voice. "Just had a question."

"I'll give you an answer if I got one. No charge," he says.

"How many of these have I had?" I ask, motioning my head towards the shot glass.

The man raises an eyebrow at me. "You shittin' me, pal? This some kind of joke?"

I shake my head. "No joke. How many?"

The bartender gives me a look that's one part pity

and one part disgust. He turns away but says as he goes, "Finish that one and then hit the road, bud."

Hit the road. Yes! That's a great fucking idea! That's exactly what I'm going to do. I leave the rye untouched on the bar and hop down from my stool. I don't even take time to grab the fiver I'd placed on the bar in anticipation of my next drink.

I don't run for the exit, but I sure as shit think about it. I get to the door and push it open, hoping to break this fucking cycle. As I take a step outside of McGillicuddy's, I draw in a deep breath and savor the taste of fresh air and freedom. I'm out!

Stepping from the curb, I hear a horn and my wind is sucked out of my lungs as something crashes into me. It should hurt, but I feel nothing. There's no time for the pain receptors in my brain to register so much as a blip. The next thing I know, I'm lying prone on the road.

Then everything goes dark.

* * *

It goes: the disorientation isn't so bad this time. I think I'm getting used to all this crazy looping. I still don't understand it. I still don't like it. But it beats the alternative, which is permanent death. Maybe this will keep happening until I figure out a way of stayin' alive. Suddenly, the Bee Gee's song worms its way into my brain and maybe that's a fate worse than death.

Scampering down from my stool, I scan the joint, trying to figure out my next move. Hide? Find something to fight back with? Fuck no. I'm no fighter. Especially not against two guys with shotguns. Back to the bathroom? I shudder at the thought. I died there once already, even if it was due to my own stupidity. I don't want to die there again.

I don't want to die anywhere again.

That's when the door to the joint bursts open and two men wearing ski masks rush in. What? No! I should have more time. I'm standing out in the open. This is no good!

The first guy, short and fat, has a pump action shotgun. The other, tall and lanky, is wielding a sawed off. Short and fat pumps his shotgun and yells, "Nobody move!"

Tall and lanky brushes past me, heading for the bar. He points his shotgun at the bulldog-faced bartender and shouts, "Gimme everything from the register. Empty the safe! Move your ass!"

Giving a slight nod of his head towards short and fat, bulldog-face says calmly, "He said not to move."

"Smart ass," tall and lanky says as he swings the butt of his shotgun at bulldog-face's head but the bartender takes a step back and he misses badly. Tall and lanky does a sloppy pirouette, propelled by the weight of the shotgun missing its mark. One of the patrons sitting at the bar, a bald-headed doughy-faced spark plug who looks like he was probably a Marine, leaps from his stool and tackles tall and lanky. The sawed off is knocked out of tall and lanky's grip and spirals across the subway tile floor.

The shotgun finds its way to my feet. Short and fat looks at the gun and then at me and just as he raises his pump action in my direction, bulldog-face hurls a salvo of pint glasses directly at him. The first glass misses wide, smashing against the wall behind short and fat, but the second and third both drill the gunman in the head. Neither glass shatters, but the impact is enough to catch him off guard. He instinctively pulls the trigger of his shotgun but it's now aimed at the ceiling and, thankfully, not at me. The gun erupts and the shell sends pockmarks into the ceiling and a rain of drywall onto short and fat's head.

I take advantage of the opportunity and scoop up the sawed off. With the ex-Marine still ably handling tall and lean, I take aim at short and fat and scream in what I intend to be a menacing growl, but instead sounds like a wounded kitten's cry, "Drop your gun. Now!" I wince as I hear my voice crack like a pimply-faced prepubescent teen.

Suddenly, a voice booms all around us, "What the fuck is going on? This is fucking bullshit! This isn't supposed to happen." The voice is loud. Too loud. And I have no idea where it's coming from. It's like the voice of God. And God is pissed.

"What's the problem?" another disembodied voice asks. This one is also loud but less angry, less ear-bleed inducing.

"This stupid fucking game," the voice of God says. "That NPC isn't supposed to attack the gunman. And THAT NPC isn't supposed to pick up a shotgun and point it at me! Everytime I load this level, the idiot NPCs, especially THAT one, are doing shit they're not supposed to do."

"You're still playing that stupid game? Turn it off," the softer voice says.

NPC? What the fuck? I look down at the sawed off in my hands and then at the other people in the bar. Bulldog-face shouts out, "What's an NP-"

Then everything goes dark.

JASON R. JAMES

IT TOLLS FOR THEE

"My best friend got the Knell when he was six years old. We were playing outside during recess. I remember he pissed his pants on the jungle gym, and I laughed."

Jordan Wainwright leaned forward in his chair, propping his elbows on top of his knees and folding his hands together under his chin. He was trying his best to look comfortable, but he wasn't.

It was a strange memory for Jordan to dredge up now—the kind of thing you have to think about to even think about. It felt like white noise. The memory of Ryan Murphy pissing himself on the jungle gym had settled inside Jordan's brain forty years ago, like a strand of DNA, but the memory itself was never important enough to pay attention to it. Ryan Murphy happened nearly forty years ago. Why should it matter now? God, he hated all of this.

Across from him, Dr. Kalchuk leaned back in his chair, jotting down a quick note on a yellow legal pad. Then, as he finished writing, Kalchuk seemed to stretch out his face, raising his eyebrows and dropping his jaw. It was the same facial tic after every note, and Jordan hated that, too.

Kalchuk was older—well into his fifties. He wore a pair of brown loafers and dark blue jeans to let everyone know he was just like the rest of them, but he matched his lower half with a tweed jacket, gray sweater vest, and a white button-up to remind his patients he was still a professional. The half moon glasses balanced on the bridge of his nose…? Those were just pretentious, but if nothing else, the doctor was comfortable being who he was.

Jordan had been seeing Kalchuk for over a year, and every week it was the same aesthetic in a different shade of boring. Maybe the repetition of outfits was supposed to put his patients at ease—if so, it was a neat trick—and it might have worked, too, if Kalchuk only had a different set of chairs in his office.

The two leather armchairs arranged so that they were facing each other at the center of the room were too soft to sit in. Every time Jordan sat down for a session he felt like he was being swallowed alive, and then he spent the rest of the hour clawing his way back to the surface—more cardio than catharsis.

Kalchuk underlined something on the legal pad and stretched his face again. Jordan pushed his shoulders back against the armchair and inched closer to the edge of the seat.

"That must have been difficult," Kalchuk finally mused, laying the legal pad down in his lap. "Getting the Knell when you're only six-years old. Knowing your best friend is going to die by the time they're twelve."

"We weren't friends after that," Jordan said.

Kalchuk lifted his notepad and started to write again. "I'm sorry to hear that, but it can be difficult after the Knell—maintaining normal relationships…especially for children your age."

"That wasn't it," Jordan shook his head. "Ryan's parents pulled him out of school after he got it. His dad was fucking rich. He quit his job, and they all drove across country together. They took Ryan to every national park

141

in the country, and they went to Disney World—twice. Then they were sailing around the world. I think Ryan drowned swimming off of Bali or something. Lucky."

Kalchuk wrote another note and stretched his face. "Lucky how? That he got to see the world before he died? Is that something you would like to do?"

Jordan bit his tongue—literally—just enough to stop himself from speaking. It was a stupid question from Kalchuk, and Jordan firmly believed that stupid questions deserved asshole answers…just maybe not when you're paying the guy to listen.

Ryan Murphy wasn't lucky because he got to see the world. It was because he skipped Generation Death—those terrible in-between years when you know you're going to get too old to live off your parents, but not old enough to start a real life of your own. Anyone who got their Knell between the ages of fifteen and twenty four fit the bill…Jordan fit *that* bill. Generation Death was the whole fucking reason he was here.

"You still can, you know. It's not too late." Kalchuk smiled. "You're not dead yet."

"I would need a passport."

Kalchuk's smile dropped. "Yeah. I guess you would. That's true." He wrote another note to himself on the legal pad. "It occurs to me, Jordan, that in all our time together, you've never talked about *your* Death Knell. You think maybe we should—"

"I don't like to talk about it."

Kalchuk smirked. "Most people come to a therapist to talk about precisely that—what they *don't* like to talk about. Maybe you should give it a try."

Jordan knew well enough that nobody liked talking about their own Knell, but he was also convinced his story was objectively worse. For starters, it happened on his birthday....

Nicole had made all the arrangements for his birthday celebration. The only thing Jordan knew for certain was that he was supposed to wear his best suit, and he should be ready to leave his apartment at 6:00 sharp. True to her word, at five of six, Nicole knocked on his door.

"You ready to have the best birthday ever?" she sang out as he opened the door.

Nicole showed up wearing her black sleeveless dress, the same one she bought for her Sorority formal, and her dark blonde hair was curled and pinned up on top of her head. Then she flashed a smile at Jordan, obviously pleased with the effect she had wrought.

"Well?" she cooed. "What do you think?"

Jordan rubbed his hand across the back of his neck. "I think we don't have to go anywhere and this would still be the best birthday ever."

Nicole shook her head at him. "That may be true, but you're not gonna want to miss this. Come on."

Their first stop that night was Huck's Tavern overlooking the river for a round of pre-dinner drinks. Nicole had reserved them a table by the window so they could see the water.

"I want you to order a martini like you're some kind of big shot lawyer. I want to be able to picture you going out for drinks with your friends in the city," Nicole said, a hint of laughter playing in her voice.

Jordan shook his head. "But I'm not any kind of lawyer yet, big shot or otherwise. Think that means I gotta stick with beer tonight."

"But you will be. I *know* you will." Nicole reached inside her purse, and pulled out a small gift box, sliding it across the linen tablecloth. "That's why I got you this. You need to look the part."

Jordan unwrapped the present, and inside he found a silver dive watch with a royal blue face. It was exactly the watch he would have picked for himself.

"Nic, you shouldn't have— This is too much." Jordan said, even as he fastened the silver watchband over his wrist.

"It's a birthday *and* a graduation present. You deserve it." Nicole blushed. "Besides, I need you to know what time it is so you don't miss any of my calls." Nicole laughed again, but Jordan understood it was only half a joke.

Their next stop for the evening was Wokano's— Jordan's favorite. It was one of those Japanese steakhouses where they cook the food right on top of the table.

"I tried to get us our own private table," Nicole said, "but they don't do that."

Jordan shrugged. "It's fine—" He caught himself. "I mean it's perfect."

Jordan didn't really get nervous until they finally sat down at the table. It was true that he didn't know *exactly* what Nicole had planned for them, but he was sure it would be fancy, and Jordan had made plans of his own.

He had met Nicole almost two years ago during Fall Semester. By Christmas Break, they were officially together, and after that, everything in Jordan's life just got better—better grades, better health, better friends, a better Jordan! He would be some kind of fool to walk away from all that now.

Jordan wasn't ready for marriage—not yet—but he could still ask Nicole to move in with him. He had a second key made for his apartment weeks ago, and tonight it was wrapped in a box and tucked inside his jacket pocket. He would give it to Nicole during dessert, sliding the box across the table just like she had done with his watch. He never had any doubt she would say "yes."

Then he got the Knell.

Kalchuk cleared his throat. "Jordan, what happened when you got—"

"I threw up. I was out with Nicole celebrating my birthday, and I threw up over everything."

Kalchuk took down a note, never looking up from his legal pad. "That's a normal reaction, you know. Most people have a physical response when they—"

"It landed on the hibachi. It started sizzling."

Kalchuk took another note.

Of course Nicole handled everything perfectly. She took Jordan home, cleaned him up, and spent the night with him while he oscillated between fits of sleep and uncontrollable sobbing. The next morning, he gave her the key to his apartment, and an easy way out.

"I want us to stay together," he said, "but I also thought we'd have a lot more time. I know last night changes everything."

Nicole reached across to take his hand. "Why should it? If we only get twenty two years together, I want to spend all of them with you."

Kalchuk folded his hands on top of the legal pad. "And how is Nicole?"

Jordan could feel a wave of warm blood surge into his fingertips and rise in his neck. It felt like he was embarrassed by the question...only it was worse than that. He looked down at the rectangle of worn carpet between his feet.

"I don't know," he muttered.

Kalchuk shifted his weight in his chair. "Last week you said you wanted to talk to her. You said—"

"I didn't call her. I don't have her number anymore."

"Did you look for it? We have something these days called the internet."

Jordan raised his eyes, the embarrassment he felt before transmuted into anger. Across from him, Kalchuk waited, his pen hovering over the legal pad.

"It was twenty years ago," Jordan whispered.

"What's that?" Kalchuck pressed.

"I said, she's the one who left me. Remember that part?"

"Yes, but she's not the one who's running out of time."

Then, for a long moment, silence hung between them.

Kalchuk was the one who finally restarted. "Your birthday's only two weeks away. Have you made any plans for your big day?"

"I've had the same plans for the last two years." Jordan forced a smile. "I'm going to dinner at Noma with a couple of friends from work. I made the reservations as soon as they opened for business."

"Oh, that's perfect," Kalchuk chimed. "What day is it you're going?"

Jordan knit his eyebrows. "What do you mean? I told you it's for my birthday."

Kalchuk looked up from the yellow legal pad. He didn't write anything. Then for a second time, an uneasy quiet settled between them.

Finally Kalchuk said, "But you mean you're going the day before?"

Jordan shook his head. "No. We're going *on* my birthday. Why—?"

Kalchuk moved forward to the edge of his seat. "What time is your reservation? What time— What if it happens before you get to the dinner? What if it happens *at* the dinner?"

Jordan's eyebrows softened and his mouth fell slightly open as the full weight of his blunder crashed over him. No one makes plans for the day it happens. It's always the day before. Why had he...?

"Maybe you can still change the reservation," Kalchuk offered.

"I don't think so," Jordan's voice was hollow.

Kalchuk held the legal pad down in his lap. He hadn't written any notes for several minutes. "Maybe you can plan a second party for the night before. You think your friends would go out two nights in a row? Worth a try, right?"

Jordan nodded.

"Good." Kalchuk put the cap on his pen, laid it down on top of his legal pad, and put the pen and pad off to one side. "We can talk about it next week if you want. Same time?"

Jordan kept nodding. "Yeah." He took hold of the arms of the chair, and with more effort than he would've liked, he leveraged himself onto his feet. "Next week sounds good."

Jacquelyn Tiger-Williams

Broken Big Sky

Hugo Sparks wished only for his father to have a warning signal like the town's tornado siren. How helpful it would be to receive a shrieking warning from afar that dad was on the way home with the stench of alcohol that was so much more than a hint and that glassy look in his eyes that was as far away as it was angry.

Take shelter. Danger is near.

Instead, eight-year-old Hugo was lucky to hear the slam of a car door that would make him at once freeze then immediately spring into action, darting to his bed, flinging the washed-out navy, baseball themed comforter over him, and faking sleep. He took special care to steady his breathing and relax his face, even as the rest of his body shouted out warnings to him.

Hugo had learned the hard way early on not to bother with turning out the lights. It was a dead give away to his dad as, upon arrival, he could see the bedroom light on in the window from the gravel driveway and then, once inside, see it had been turned off when darkness peeked out from beneath Hugo's bedroom door. And so Hugo went to bed each night in his well-lit room, despite having little fear of the dark. His father's occasional jeers about this fake phobia were nothing compared to being found awake on the tornado nights. Hugo would choose his father's harsh words over his hard hands any day.

The truth was that the tornado nights were just as infrequent as actual twisters. Hugo couldn't make sense of why, quite out of nowhere, his father would cloud over and just head out for the night. Hugo, a boy of logic, knew that tornadoes were not a random occurrence. Specific conditions needed to occur in tandem for a twister to increase in likelihood. It frustrated Hugo that he could not identify the conditions that set his father off on his own twisting path.

Some nights, having finally arrived back home, his father would lean over the sleeping child, his hot breath blanketing Hugo's sandy brown curls and perfectly freckled skin. Six-year-old and seven-year-old Hugo had previously perfected the art of the relaxed sleeping face, having carefully studied the details of his mother's sleeping face when she dozed off on the couch as well as the face of his baby cousin they occasionally babysat. He even practiced it in the bathroom mirror, perched up on the faux marble counter, "sleeping" but with one eye open to carefully examine his progress in the mirror. The challenge was to open that eye ever so gently so as not to contort the rest of his face.

On this particular night, Hugo was laying on his belly building with his legos on the royal blue rug in his bedroom. He played alone quietly, humming periodically to himself as he focused on the spaceship he was constructing. Hugo could hear the thrumming of the heater in the quiet of the room.

Hugo paused at the sound of wheels on the gravel driveway, head tilted slightly to the side as he listened carefully. A car door slammed, louder than necessary. In one quick movement, Hugo swept the lego pieces out of the way under his bed, then hopped into bed. He inhaled deeply in and slowly let it out, settling his nerves and willing his body to relax. Hugo curled up on his side and tucked the comforter up around his shoulders. He waited.

Hugo heard the familiar sounds of his father's heavy boots walking in the front door and crossing the living room. He heard his mother's even voice, probably saying hello and that the boy was asleep. Nonetheless, the boots walked across the worn linoleum of the kitchen and down the hall to open the boy's bedroom door. Hugo put his training into action—eyes closed, face relaxed, breathing soft and steady. The knob turned and the door gave its familiar creak as it opened.

Hugo heard his mother's lighter footsteps quickly approach. Her gentle, hushed coaxing to shut the door and let the boy sleep finally worked as her husband relented and headed back down the hallway. Behind Hugo's closed eyes, he could picture his mother peeking in on him from the doorway and then easing the door shut. Now alone again in the room, Hugo rolled on to his back and breathed a sigh of relief. He listened for a few minutes more until his nervous system winded down. Hugo settled in to sleep for real, relieved by the night's peaceful ending.

Hugo's brief sleep was interrupted by the sound of angry voices. Mom and Dad were arguing. He strained to listen but couldn't make out the exact topic. Whatever it was, there was swearing by his dad as his mom tried to explain her position. Hugo knew there was no point trying to talk to him on these nights. He knew his mom knew it, too. Hugo was reminded of something a cashier at the Food Lion had said once as she shook her head, watching two customers argue over a box of Ritz crackers. "Sometimes people are just fixing to fight."

The voices of Hugo's parents ebbed and flowed for a while as the argument continued. Hugo heard the banging of pots being put in the sink with too much enthusiasm. He knew that was his mother, who often cleaned when upset. He heard the slamming of cabinet doors which was his dad's signature move. And then a loud thud. What was that? Hugo leaned up on his elbow, listening carefully as he worked his way down the mental list of familiar sounds of home, never landing on what that loud thud could be.

Hugo then heard an especially powerful slam of his parents' bedroom door. Finally. His father rarely came back out once he headed to his bedroom for the night.

Hugo listened for his mother. He could hear her murmuring for a few minutes. It sounded as though her feet were shuffling around on the kitchen floor. That's odd, Hugo thought, thinking of her usual quick, gentle steps. Hugo continued to listen until the house got quiet. She must have settled down to sleep on the couch. She probably didn't want to be near Hugo's father either. Hugo followed suit and got himself comfortable again. He drifted off to sleep, grateful things had settled relatively quickly.

Hugo woke up rested, but confused. The sun was shining in brightly, too brightly, through the edges of his window shade. His mother should've woken him for school by now. He peered at his small alarm clock on the worn, engineered wood top of his night table that read 9:47. Hugo furrowed his eyebrows and swung his legs over the edge of his bed. Today was the day he'd do his state presentation for social studies in front of the class. He had carefully written out his note cards and practiced over and over. Last night at dinner, Mom had said he would nail the speech. Dad had laughed and said even he could nail the speech at this point because he'd heard it so many times. Mom had ironed his shirt with the collar that

Hugo hated even if it did make him feel like a grown up. Why hadn't she woken him? Hugo opened his bedroom door and gave his eyes a moment to adjust to the darker hallway. He noted his parents' bedroom door was still closed, a sign that his father was still sleeping. He padded down the hall, still wondering why Mom hadn't woken him and if Miss Simpson would be upset that he was late for school.

Hugo stopped abruptly at the entrance to the kitchen.

She was sitting on the floor, her back resting against the oven, but sort of slouched. She would never let him slouch like that. Sit up, Hugo, she'd say. Straight and tall like a superhero.

Hugo bent down a bit, leaning to the side, to peer at Mom's face. Though some of her hair was in front of her face, he could see her eyes were closed. Why would she be sleeping in the kitchen? For a moment, he considered if she was fake sleeping but quickly discounted that seeing as she didn't know about his secret fake sleeping abilities. Hugo tentatively crossed the kitchen and crouched down beside her leg, his palms resting on the knees of his Spiderman pajama pants. He reached one hand out and gently touched her arm to wake her. Hugo quickly pulled his hand back, startled by the chill of her skin in the warm kitchen.

Montana's nickname is the Treasure State.

"Momma?" Hugo whispered in the aching silence that filled the kitchen.

The capital of Montana is Helena.

Hugo stretched his arm out to move her brown hair away from her face. Noticing a bit of blood that had run from her ear down her cheek, he gasped and pulled his hand back, tucking his arm against his chest.

Montana's state bird is the western meadowlark.

Hugo lost his balance, stumbling back and landing on his bottom. He scrambled himself farther away, never taking his eyes off his mother, until his back was up against the kitchen wall. Though his body could go no farther, Hugo's feet continued frantically trying to crabwalk him backwards, away from the unthinkable.

The state flower of Montana is bitterroot. It has purplish-pink petals.

Hugo's breathing was ragged. A dull roaring filled his head, not unlike water rushing and tumbling over a waterfall.

Montana's state animal is the grizzly bear. The state tree is the ponderosa pine.

Over the rushing water, Hugo heard his own heart hammering in his ears.

Montana is well known for its glaciers and the Rocky Mountains. Many people call Montana Big Sky Country because of its beautiful, wide open views.

Hugo scrambled for the front door and ran for Miss Nicole next door.

His neighbor opened her door to find Hugo trembling and silently crying, unable to speak. When she saw he had wet himself, she was sure something was terribly wrong. She grabbed her phone, scooped Hugo up in her arms, and raced across both their driveways for his home. Carefully placing him down on the dark green plastic chair by his door, she stepped in to find what she had feared may come one day. Her dear friend gone. Nicole raced back outside, picked up Hugo, and ran for her place. Inside, she bolted the door, called the police, and cradled that sweet boy in her lap, gently rocking him as she nuzzled her face in his hair, breathing in the most beautiful thing her friend had ever created. Only then did Hugo finally make a sound, letting out a guttural wail.

Kara Knauss

MAYBE THE MUSES

Maybe the muses are not so far
But rather familiar.
Roots from an ancestral tree
Twisted with Common bone
Flowing intimate blood throughout.
With boughs strong enough
     to hold our weight,
     to give us shelter,
So we stretch out and rest.

Listen to the squirrel's chatter.
The sound collides with snow-strung air,
Bird-song whispers on wind
Born by laughter from our middle.
A web glistens with the soft gleam of light

That pushes through the gray sky.
It comes from all around.

When the circle gets built by your grandfather's hands,
An arrow is shot across time
And caught in my eager fist.
I scrawl a new story on parchment—
    A map, meant for a peregrine's leg.

Game Over

ABOUT THE AUTHORS

D. W. Oravic crafts mature, character-driven speculative fiction from his home in Philadelphia, PA, with a particular affinity towards strong but complex female protagonists. While his settings are unconstrained, his stories are entirely human; Oravic wants to know what makes his characters tick and squeezes them to their limit. Oravic is a biological research specialist at the University of Pennsylvania and has been a member of the Pitman Writers Guild since 2021.

T. S. DeBrosse is an author, educator, and editor. She is the author of *The Hazy Souls* series, a fantasy that follows the cosmic awakening of a troubled prince as the world descends into apocalypse. DeBrosse's stories are predominantly character-driven, with events that explore how neuropsychological processes underpin mysticism, balancing moments of action, horror, and comedy. You can find out more about her work at www.tsdebrosse.com.

J.D. Marshall is a longtime fan of fantasy, sci-fi, and horror. He's an avid player and gamemaster of tabletop role-playing games and has published several adventures. He believes that the neurological difference between fiction and reality is slight, and by telling and reading stories, we can induce internal change.

Jenna Rentzel has been a member of the Pitman Writers' Guild since 2019. As a teacher she always felt that stories were some of the best ways to make lasting connections, learn about the world, and discover oneself. She loves all types of fiction, but has a special place in her heart for young adult and middle grade fiction.

Michael Shaw writes about strange worlds, quirky and colorful characters, and bizarre and unusual situations featuring elements of the inexplicable, improbable, and downright impossible. Michael is a co-founder and inaugural President of Pitman Writers' Guild and Secretary of the Delaware Valley Chapter, Sisters in Crime. In 2021, Michael was honored with the Leon B. Burstein / Mystery Writers of America Scholarship for Mystery Writers. Originally from Springfield, Delaware County, Pennsylvania, Michael currently resides in Pitman, New Jersey with his wife, Ashley, their two dogs; Eleanor Roosevelt and Bogart, and two cats; Gatsby and Voodoo. Visit Michael's webpage at www.MichaelShawAuthor.com.

Jason R. James is a founding member of the Pitman Writers' Guild. He enjoys writing in most genres, but gravitates towards fantasy and science fiction. He is the author of the ANOM series as well as the middle-grade fantasy series: The Rainbow Princess Chronicles. Jason's all-time favorite novel is *The Black Cauldron* by Lloyd Alexander.

Jacquelyn Tiger-Williams is a fifth-grade teacher. As she spends the bulk of her time with the under 12 set, she loves to read and write middle grade fiction. Jacki relishes those brass ring stories that change a person's view of the world and she strives to write the same for kids. Jacki weaves her connection to nature and animals into her work. She also crafts essays reflecting on cultural and life events.

Kara Knauss is a founding member of the Pitman Writers' Guild. She is a proud member of the LGBTQIA+ community, and is curious about human connection and emotional interaction. It's impossible to choose a single genre of writing as Kara's favorite, but she's explored her creativity in fantasy, magical realism, contemporary fiction, and poetry.

Viral Cat

Art Eclectic

Follow us online
www.viralcathouse.com

Follow us online
www.pitmanwrites.com